INCA THE GOLDEN SUN

Also by Peachill:

Red Eagle: A Native American
Barka: Lion of Carthage
1453: The Last Days of Constantinople
Empress Wu: Rise

INCA THE GOLDEN SUN

peachill

Peachill Publishing
Chapel Hill | New York | Santa Monica
www.peachill.com

First published by Peachill Publishing LLC, 2016

Peachill Publishing asserts to moral write to be identified as the author of this work

A catalogue record for this book is available from the US Library of Congress

ISBN [insert ISBN given for correct format]

Printed by [placeholder] [if printed format]

All rights reserved. No part of this publication may be reproduced, stored in a retrieval system, or transmitted, in any form or by any means, electronic, mechanical, photocopying, recording, or otherwise, without prior permission of the publisher.

Preface

Peachill is a collaborative community of artists and regular folks who are passionate about telling authentic stories about the world we live in. We believe in a few key principles that collectively make Peachill unique:

- Creativity is an integral part of what makes us human
- Anyone can be creative
- Freelancers all over the globe are ready to make great stories together
- Regular folks want to be involved in the collaboration

We are creative animals. The act of building something new, creating something from scratch, and having a vision for the world around us is a key part of what makes us human beings. In anthropology, art is used as one of the earliest signs of civilization and it continues to be a key indicator of human progress. In neuroscience, creativity is observed as a key link to happiness and stress-relief. This is because creative pulls us out of the monotony of everyday, where our thoughts and desires are the most important thing in the universe, and gives us the perspective to be feel a part of something larger than ourselves, part of a story, part of the human race, part of the world. This is the state of greatest satisfaction for human existence, and creativity helps us get there. It is our magic carpet ride.

Everyone is creative. In our own way, sparks of creativity fly off of each of us every day of our lives. Not everyone pays attention to these moments, and even fewer have the time to dedicate significant time to purely "creative" projects, but that doesn't stop each of us from having the ability to create. Additionally, no one is creative in a silo. Even traditional authors, whose names are printed alone on the book cover, benefit greatly from freely shared ideas. They choose the ideas that fit, discard those that don't, and change others to fit their vision. Whether every artist will admit it or not, creativity is inherently a collaborative process. At Peachill, we are transparent in our belief of artistic collaboration. You will not see a single "author" name on our cover. This book has been a team effort and could not have happened any other way. We do not see this as a radical change in creative method but rather an honest admission of art in general.

The freelancer community around the world is large and growing. We believe freelancers are at their best when offered a structured approach to deliver the work they love. We believe excellent talent is hidden in corners that are often overlooked - young talent, international talent, career-switchers. At Peachill, all we care about is quality. We are passionate about developing talented professionals and helping them achieve their ultimate goals as artists. This process not only creates a fulfilling and mutually beneficial relationship between the platform and collaborators, but it ensures a fresh flow of ideas and approaches to the work itself. We do not believe that we have the creative answer to every decision, but together we have a better shot.

Freelancers aren't the only ones who want to be involved in the creative process. What about fans? What about creative individuals who are passionate about projects but do not have the time to dedicate on a full-time basis? We do not believe that such collaborators should be left out in the cold. Peachill offers an online platform where freelancers and collaborators can trade meaningful interactions throughout the process. The platform offers the opportunity for collaborators to vote on project ideas, fund fully developed story boards, participate in key junctures of the creative process, and hear directly from the creative team as the project comes together. This collaborative approach is betting on a desire for more people to have a say in the art they are consuming, without demanding too much time. This platform will continue to evolve to create the best experience for all participants, while not sacrificing quality or transparency. We intend for all collaborators to feel real ownership in the projects in which they are involved. We intend to give credit and acknowledgement both online and within the stories themselves. And we intend for collaborators to tell their friends and help us sell these stories so that we can fund more projects in the future.

This book is a product of that environment. We hope you enjoy it.

PART ONE

CHAPTER ONE

Cajamarca, the Incan Empire, 1532

Francisco Pizarro stood in the shadows at the end of the courtyard, watching the birds circle the cloudy sky. With their feathers divided between large patches of black and white, the birds looked as if they had been cut from a chessboard. Playing pieces in the games of God and men.

"What are those?" Pizarro pointed at the birds.

"My lord?" Friar Vicente turned from watching the procession approaching them up the hillside.

"The birds," Pizarro asked sharply. Fifty years of hard labor and hard living had whittled away anything spare in his body or his mind. He had no patience for those who would waste what time remained. "Tell me."

"Caracara, I believe." The friar squinted, even more wrinkles filling his already crumpled face. "Scavengers. They feast off corpses."

"How fitting," Pizarro said.

The friar opened his mouth as if to respond, then seemed to think better of it.

Pizarro tipped his head from side to side, loosening out the muscles in his neck. He bent his knees and rolled his shoulders, careful not to scrape himself on the edges of his armored breastplate. If there were to be trouble, then he would be ready, and if it all went to plan, there would be trouble.

The procession of savages arrived at the far edge of the village. There were hundreds of them, wearing white tunics decorated in red, blue, and black; the colors were in bold blocks like those of the caracara feathers. Some carried long handled axes, others clubs and rectangular shields decorated in the same abstract patterns as their clothing. Those in the lead wore golden helmets with red feathers protruding from their peaks. All were muscular and intimidating, their skin pale brown, hair straight and black, expressions marked with scars. They chanted as they marched, an unsettling chorus that Pizarro could not understand but that sent a shiver down his spine.

The strangeness of the procession only made the town seem more unimpressive. A collection of rough stone huts, no better than those of the village where Pizarro had grown up, half a world and a whole lifetime away in Spain. It must be a pitiful place, to be no better than that. Or perhaps this was what constituted grandeur to barbarians with no steel or civilized clothing.

The procession separated as it came into the courtyard, men peeling off to the left and right. Out of the column an even more impressive group emerged, gold jewelry heavy around their necks, the feathers of their headdresses a riot of color. They carried a litter, on which was mounted a golden throne. In it sat a man younger than Pizarro but as intimidating as any of the guards. His jewelry was of beautifully crafted gold. A helmet, earrings, a neckpiece large enough that it could have been armor, all flashed like fire when they caught the light.

"That's him?" Pizarro asked.

"The Emperor Atahualpa," said their interpreter, a nervous young man of local descent. "His soldiers are singing of his victories."

"There is only one monarch of these lands," Pizarro said. "And the King of Spain does not wear feathers like some bloated pheasant."

"You might not want to-"

Pizarro silenced the youth with a glare.

"I am no imbecile," he said. "There is a time for truth, and this will not be it."

Resisting the urge to reach for his sword, he watched as Atahualpa's warriors filled the courtyard. This was not like Panama had been, with its scattered tribes and wild beasts. There were more men standing between him and the Incan Emperor than in the whole of Pizarro's expedition.

Little did the natives know, the men of his expedition had not stepped into the open as these ignorant savages had. They lurked in the shadows of the buildings surrounding the courtyard, on the rooftops above, and behind the shutters of these ramshackle houses. Watching and waiting, guns ready. Behind him were hidden cannons, ready to smash these primitives to pulp. Every one of his men would be eyeing this display of wealth as eagerly as he did, counting the gold helmets and the fat disks of earrings, calculating their share.

At last, his time had come. Soon he would not just be wealthy — a goal he had long ago achieved — he would be rich beyond the dreams of youth, a man of fame and power, and the victor who brought another savage empire to heel.

"Hernando?" He spoke quietly, not looking at the woodpile behind which his youngest brother lurked, with a sword in his hand and a grin on his face, helmet tipped at a rakish angle. "Are the men ready?"

"As God is our witness," Hernando said, softly enough that only Pizarro and the friar could hear. As if to prove the point there was a click from the building behind them, the sound of flint and steel sparking tinder ready for a cannon's fuse.

"Good," Pizarro said. "If I'm taken don't hesitate — attack, and to hell with these pagans."

"But what of you?" Hernando asked.

"I carry God's blessing, the King's favor, and the finest armor money can buy." Pizarro rapped a knuckle against his breastplate. "Between them, they will keep me safe. Fortune favors the brave, and I want all the fortune in the world."

At last, the chanting stopped. Only the throne bearers were still moving, bringing Atahualpa to the head of his force. He looked down at the Spaniards with dark eyes so intense they seemed about to pierce the veil of Pizarro's body and look straight into the depths of his soul. Stern and expectant, the Emperor waited.

Pizarro had met prouder men. He would not be intimidated by the tricks nobles used to keep small men in line. Francisco Pizarro was no small man.

"Come, reverend Father," he said. "Let us bring these savages the King's greeting."

He strode out of the shadows, the friar walking nervously beside him, and approached the Emperor of the Incas.

Above their heads, the caracara wheeled and soared.

CHAPTER TWO

Western Spain, Years Before

Francisco crouched in the dust at the corner of the street, his over-sized and ragged clothes crumpled around him. He watched as an old man hobbled along the dirt road, a stick in one hand and a sack in the other. A pouch hung from his belt, not fat with gold like those of merchants, but fat enough that there must be something worthwhile inside.

Pressing his thumb against the blade, Francisco tested the edge of his knife. It would have seemed tiny in the hands of a grown up, but to him it was a deadly weapon and a path to getting fed. Not big enough for him to menace the old man or take him in a fight — at five years old, Francisco wasn't going to be picking fights with anyone. But a knife had other uses.

The old man walked slowly, limping off his right leg. His head tilted away a little, as if he didn't want to look toward his own injured side. That would make it harder for him to see Francisco coming, as long as he waited long enough to pounce.

The wait seemed eternal, as it often did when waiting for adults to do anything. Time sped by, and yet they seemed content to let it go. It frustrated Francisco. But at last the old man was passing the shadows in which the boy sat, his head turned away.

Fast as a diving hawk, Francisco darted out. With his empty hand he grabbed the pouch, while with the other he hooked the knife through its strings. Hours of sharpening the blade paid off. The chords gave way like butter in a hot sun. Pouch in hand, he rushed back along the street and into an alley between two leaning stone buildings.

"Cutpurse!" the old man bellowed. "Vagabond! Someone help me!"

The sound of heavy footsteps announced that the alarm had been raised. Francisco cursed himself for not being more subtle, more agile. For letting the old man realize what had happened. He would practice for next time. He would make his blade sharper.

If there was to be a next time then he needed to hide. He couldn't outrun a mob of the town's honest men.

There was a well in the open space between some of the houses. Behind it was a stand on which women rested their buckets while they chattered. Water had eroded the ground beneath it, leaving a gap beneath the planks. A gap too small for a grown man, but just large enough for a five-year-old.

The sun-baked earth scraped the skin from Francisco's knees and elbows as he wormed his way beneath the boards. He could hear the sound of men striding down the street toward him. With one last desperate push he wriggled forward and out of sight.

There was just enough space for him to twist onto his back. Peering out, he saw men with swords striding around, shouting to each other, telling each other where he wasn't. As they disappeared from view and the excitement of the chase wore off, Francisco felt his eyelids drooping. Beneath the shade of the planks, he fell asleep.

∼

As evening was falling he woke from a dream of gold and distant forests. A pair of adults was walking past, a man and a woman giggling together as they headed out into the fields. Francisco wondered what could be so funny. Perhaps they were just better fed than he was. It was easier to laugh when you weren't hungry.

His own hunger was so great it had become a pain in his belly. Desperate to end it, he waited no longer to see if the coast was clear but wriggled out into the dusk. Through the growing gloom, he made his way toward a house on the edge of town.

It was an old house, still standing thanks to the care with which its stonewalls had been constructed, though little effort had been made to maintain it. Creepers grew up one side and light spilt out through gaps in the walls. A man in a leather tunic stood by the back door, a club in his hand and a scowl on his scarred face.

"I want to see Blind Garcia," Francisco said.

"One of his little recruits, huh?" The guard sneered but stepped aside, opening the door and ushering Francisco in.

A wall of sound hit him as he crossed the threshold. Men and women laughing and shouting. The clatter of cups and jugs. The rattle of dice on a table.

The interior of the building was well lit. A fire blazed in

the hearth despite the summer heat, and tall candles were lit in nooks and on shelves. Big white candles, like the ones Francisco had seen in church. All around, men and women sat at tables improvised from barrels and planks. Some were playing games with knives, dice, or knucklebones. Many of the women sat in the men's laps; their dresses unfastened to the waist. Everyone was drinking. The stench of sweat and cheap red wine made Francisco's head spin.

Everyone was happy. Everyone had what they wanted. Everyone except Francisco.

Weaving between the revelers, he made his way to a corner of the room where a grey-haired man in ragged black robes sat behind a table, his milky eyes staring sightlessly at the cup in front of him.

"That you, Francisco?" Blind Garcia asked.

Francisco stood amazed, as he always did, at Garcia's ability to recognize him before he spoke. He nodded, then realized how useless that was.

"Yes," he said, reaching up to place the pouch on the table. "Got this."

Blind Garcia tipped out the contents of the pouch. He raised an eyebrow as he picked up each coin in turn, feeling its weight and inscription.

"Not bad, little Pizarro," he said. "Not good, but not bad."

Garcia raised a hand and a man in a stained apron appeared at his side. That was another way that Garcia amazed Francisco — the ability to make people come to him and give him the things he wanted. This must be what life was like for his uncles and cousins as well, though unlike Garcia they would not share their lives with Francisco.

"Bring the boy porridge," Garcia said. "No meat today — he'll need to do better for that."

A moment later Francisco was holding a bowl and a spoon. He retreated to a safe corner, huddling protectively over his porridge, and gobbled it down. As he did so, he dreamed of being a powerful man, like Garcia or those uncles who kept pretending that Francisco didn't exist. A man people brought food for. A man people brought gold for. A man who never went hungry.

As he swallowed the last of the porridge, his eyelids once again drooping despite the noise all around him, he made himself a promise: One day he would be one of those powerful men.

Leaning in his shadowy corner, Francisco Pizarro fell asleep.

CHAPTER THREE

Trujillo, Spain

The friar's wagon bounced along the rutted dirt roads. No one took care to maintain the ways between towns out here. It was not an important part of the kingdom but a backwater as neglected as Francisco himself.

The rugged hills around Trujillo were dotted with small, hardy trees, dark green against the dried out grass and struggling crops. It had been a hard year, with little rain to break up the blazing sunshine. On a hill above the road, sails turned listlessly on the squat white tower of a windmill, though Francisco doubted there was grain to grind.

He wished that the friar had been more tuneful. All the way across the backcountry, the priest had been singing tunelessly to himself, while Francisco suffered in silence beneath a pile of wool robes in the back. He could hardly complain — doing so would have told the friar that he was there and lost him his transport. Besides, it was not much farther now. The town of Trujillo was ahead of them, less than half a mile away.

Trujillo seemed huge compared with Blind Garcia's village. Houses covered an area the size of many farms, crowded in together as tightly as men in a tavern on feast day. A tall church loomed out of the center, its bell ringing for midday.

The wagon rolled into town and Francisco slid out the back, ducking into an alleyway before anyone could pay him any attention. There were so many people that it made hiding easier. They couldn't possibly all know each other, and the crowds were busy enough for him to become lost between their legs.

It took a few false turns, but at last he found himself in a familiar, quiet street. He walked up to the nondescript door of one of the whitewashed houses. Heart in his throat, he raised his hand.

He hesitated. What if he had the wrong door? What if she wasn't there? What if she had died? He didn't think he could live with that.

This wasn't the way powerful men behaved. They acted decisively. Blind Garcia had told him so.

Francisco took a deep breath and knocked as hard as he could.

After a few moments, he heard footsteps. The door creaked open and a middle-aged woman looked down at him. She wore plain but clean clothes, more mended than they had been when last he saw her. As she lowered her gaze to look at him, her expression turned quickly from one of welcome to a look of shock.

There was a bang as she slammed the door in his face. Footsteps shuffled away.

He sagged. So much effort, all for this. No one gave him what he wanted. The world never bent to his will.

Feeling powerless and alone, Francisco turned and walked

slowly back up the street.

Behind him the door creaked open. He turned in amazement and saw her standing there, a small loaf of bread in her hands. With a nervous glance around, she waved him over.

"Here." She thrust the bread at him.

Famished from long days on the road, with little chance to either steal or buy a meal, Francisco tore into the loaf, barely chewing before he swallowed each mouthful.

"You can't be here," she said. "If my husband sees you he will beat me, and then he will leave me."

Francisco nodded sadly. He knew what it was to be beaten and what it was to be deserted. Of course, she did not want to be seen with him. It hurt, but she had to survive, just as he did. And she had given him this bread, still warm from the oven.

Clutching the loaf to him, he tried to muster the words for what he was feeling. He didn't understand the hammering of his heart or the tightness in his chest. He didn't know how to say even the parts that made sense to him. But he knew, as he felt its rough crust between his fingers that this was the most important loaf of bread he had ever eaten.

"Thank you, Mother," he said, looking up at her with wide eyes.

For a moment she hesitated, and he saw something shining, the beginnings of tears that would not flow. Then she shut the door again, and he heard her rushing away. Someone nearby was sobbing.

Turning once again, Francisco padded away. He kept eating as he went, not wanting to risk the chance of a bigger boy taking his food from him. As he reached the end of the quiet little street, he enjoyed the rare feeling of a truly full stomach. He should have felt happy, but as he looked back at that anonymous door, he felt something else, like a weight pressing upon his chest. If there was a word for this feeling then he didn't know it. He was sure of only one thing — that he would never see his mother again.

CHAPTER FOUR

Cuzco, the Incan Empire

The ball hit the wall and bounced away with a satisfying thud. Atahualpa ran after it, reaching out with the stick he'd carefully chosen for his game. If he'd been a little taller he could have reached the branch he really wanted — even at ten years old, he was strong enough to break it off. But it had been out of reach, and so he had made do with this one.

He knocked the ball back toward the wall, careful not to hit the piles of pots around the square. Most people were busy in the fields or workshops, the courtiers supervising the servants and laborers, leaving this space for him to play in. It was good to be left alone for once, in peace. There was little peace when you were the Emperor's son.

"Atahualpa!" Huascar appeared at the end of the square. He waved a stick of his own. "What are you doing?"

Atahualpa hesitated. His half-brother sometimes judged and mocked him, as older siblings often did. But he was better company when there was no one around, no courtiers or girls to show off to.

"I made up a game." Atahualpa picked up the ball, showing it to Huascar as the other boy approached. "A trader brought this. He said that the Aztecs use it for sport. He didn't know the rules, so I've made my own. It is a very good game." He pointed at the large slab of stone resting against one wall, and the smoke stain on the whitewashed wall at head height above it. "If I hit the stone then I can pick up the ball and try to hit the stain. But I have to use the stick to hit the ball."

"How do I win?" Huascar peered at the ball, one eyebrow raised. With his broad features, he looked more like their father than Atahualpa did, but Atahualpa was taller and stronger despite his age. When people talked about those differences, things got difficult between them, and Huascar became more prone to mocking. Atahualpa didn't like that.

"I..." Atahualpa hadn't thought about how the game was won. When it was only him, it didn't matter. He considered saying as much, but there was a glint in Huascar's eye — his brother wouldn't be happy until he had a way to dominate. Besides, he didn't want to reveal that he had forgotten anything. Hastily, Atahualpa thought about how the game could work. "You get one point for hitting the stone, which represents the world, and two for the stain, which represents the flames of the great god Inti. Highest score wins."

"Sounds stupid," Huascar sneered, but he snatched the ball, flung it in the air and then hit it with his stick as it fell. It bounced off the wall next to the stone and rolled swiftly past Atahualpa. The boys looked at each other, grinned, and gave chase.

It was a glorious day, the sun god Inti shining down from a sky as clear and beautiful as dreams. For an hour, they chased up and down the courtyard, bouncing the ball off the wall. Atahualpa took the lead early on, but Huascar didn't give up, or stop chattering away even as he ran out of breath.

"Idiot! You can barely throw straight," he said as Atahualpa's stick caught the ball at the wrong angle, sending it off to the left. "A monkey could play this game better than you."

As the scores got further apart, the insults came thicker and faster.

"Call that running?" the red-faced Huascar shouted, though Atahualpa hadn't seen him ever try to run that fast. "You're only winning because you cheat."

At last, Huascar scored again. He grabbed the ball, flung it up in the air and hit it with all his might. The uneven end of his stick struck the ball as badly as Atahualpa had earlier. It rocketed away from them, bounced off the ground once, and hit a pile of pots by a doorway.

The two boys stood frozen as the bottom pot cracked, wobbled, then split in two, dropping the rest onto the stones with an almighty crash. Shards of pottery went everywhere.

"What was that noise?" One of the Emperor's wives strode out of the doorway, her simple blue and white dress flapping around her sandaled feet. Her expression was as fierce as any warrior. "My pots!" She glared at them. "Which of you did this?"

Both boys stood silent. They exchanged a look, one they had shared in the past. Whatever their differences, for one to give the other up would be going too far.

"Well?" The woman loomed over them, hands on her hips. "Is no one going to confess?"

As they remained silent, she turned her glare upon Atahualpa.

"It was you, wasn't it?" She grabbed him by the arm. "It's

always you causing trouble. I've seen your mother scolding you so many times it's appalling. This time you will get a proper lesson."

Her fingers hurt as they dug into his arm. He could have wriggled free. He could even have hit her — he was strong; he could have made her regret ever touching him. Except that his father was more protective of his wives than his sons. After all, boys were meant to fend for themselves. He might not have taken kindly to Atahualpa hitting one of those wives, and his wrath was a terrible thing.

As she dragged him through the doorway, Atahualpa looked back at Huascar. He mouthed the word "Please," begging his older brother to confess and spare him the consequences. Huascar remained silent.

The woman snatched up a stick from the corner of the room and raised it above Atahualpa.

"Let this be a lesson." She snapped the stick down upon his head, and his shoulders, then his back as he curled up to protect himself from the pain. "No more trouble, little prince. We are all watching you."

From outside, Atahualpa heard the sound of another stick hitting something, and of a ball bouncing against a stone slab.

CHAPTER FIVE

Barcelona, Spain

The Spanish royal residence was everything Francisco Pizarro had dreamed of since childhood. Art and sculptures from around the world decorated the walls, rich tapestries hanging between them. Courtiers stalked confidently from one room to the next, talking loudly, their ruffs extending from their necks like the plumage of magnificently strange birds. Servants slid silently between them — carrying messages, delivering drinks, ushering people to meetings or to places to stand in line. It was dazzling. It was a moment he had dreamed of for over twenty years.

Of course, in his dreams he had been another guest, not an infiltrator sneaking in off the street. The dream clothes had been specially selected so that he would stand out and attract the King's eye, ready to befriend him and impress him with tales of his exploits. The clothes he wore today had been specially selected to blend in, stolen off a courtier noted for being a nobody, just prestigious enough to tread without comment in the halls of power.

Pizarro found himself swept up in a movement of courtiers as they made their way out into a large courtyard. People stood around the sides, looking toward an arch at the end. Pizarro, stuck at the back, couldn't see what was happening and didn't want to draw attention by pushing his way to the front. Instead, he clambered up the back of a cart left by servants in the corner of the courtyard — a move that attracted a few discreet looks of disapproval — and from there watched the proceedings across the heads of the crowd.

The King sat on a throne at the side of the courtyard, his deep red robes trimmed with white fur, a jeweled crown upon his head. His face drooped in fat folds and his hooded eyes seemed half closed, yet there was an intensity to the way he leaned forward, watching as a procession emerged from the archway and strode toward him.

At the front was the man whose presence had drawn Pizarro here today — Hernan Cortez. Adventurer, conqueror, hero of Spain. Francisco's cousin.

Cortez was dressed in fine armor, a master crafted sword hanging in the jeweled scabbard at his side. A look of pride filled his fine, youthful features as he bowed before the King.

How different would things have been, Pizarro wondered bitterly, if his mother had been the famed beauty, the one who married up into society. He might have been the one before the throne today, talking of his exploits and displaying his riches. He might have been the one whose family funded him to adventure in the New World. He might have been the one famed throughout Europe for bringing the dogs of a foreign empire to heel.

"Your Majesty." Cortez faced the King, but his voice was raised, playing to the crowd. "The Aztecs have fallen. A once mighty empire of savages, brought to heel by Christian courage and Spanish steel. Like the crusaders of old, God has blessed our righteous work."

The crowd cheered and Cortez turned to acknowledge them with a look of such self-satisfaction that it made Pizarro's blood boil.

"All of this, Your Majesty, I have done in your name," Cortez continued. "A new world has been added to the Kingdom of Spain. Its people bow their knee to you. Its wealth pours across the ocean into your coffers. Its lands are yours, thanks to the boldness of our venture."

As Cortez spoke, a parade of wealth followed him into the palace. There were a dozen men and women, their skin a shade darker than that of southern Spaniards, their hair straight and black. They stared ahead of them, eyes blank in beautiful, aquiline features, the prized beauties of an exotic world. The male savages were bare chested, the women in dresses fringed with beads. All wore golden jewelry set with dazzling blue stones, which they began to remove and place before the King at a signal from Cortez. For a moment, one of them hesitated, and Cortez's hand went to his sword. Reluctantly, the man unfastened his necklace and placed it before the throne.

The crowd gasped as further spectacles followed. Beasts prowled in on long chains, giant cats with spotted skin and fearsome, snarling teeth. Then there were the chests, each one piled high with gold, statues, or cloth. Each was placed before the King, whose grin only widened.

At last, the King rose, and the murmurs of the crowd fell silent.

"Our friend Cortez brings great marvels." The King took

Cortez's hand and raised it above his head. "More than this, he has brought to heel these rebels who have defied the will of your King, our Pope, and God almighty himself, who has placed the New World in our hands. Let all witness the strength of our loyal conqueror, Hernan Cortez!"

Cortez smiled smugly as the crowd cheered, clapped their hands, and stamped their feet. All except Pizarro, who only glared at his cousin, this offspring of a branch of the family that would not acknowledge his own, never mind reach out to help them. He would make this pompous braggart regret treating them like this. What Cortez had achieved thanks to his family's wealth, Pizarro could take away with one thrust of the rusty knife on his belt.

He climbed down the back of the wagon. Under cover of the noise and bustle of applause, he started working his way through the crowd, a bitter snarl on his lips, fingers closing around the handle of his dagger.

Once again, the King raised his hands for silence.

"Hernan Cortez, before God and these witnesses, I grant upon you the position of governor of Mexico," the King said. "From now on, your blood is noble blood, as is only fitting for a man of your abilities."

The cheering became deafening. Pizarro's knuckles went white as he gripped the blade tighter. He was near the front of the crowd now. All he had to do was wait for people to start moving, for Cortez to be caught up in the bustle, and he would have his chance. He could not have what Cortez had, but he could take it away.

One row back from the front, he stopped and stared at the prisoners. They too had once had the power, wealth, and respect Cortez had, though in a foreign land. What one could gain, another could take way. There must be more like them in the measureless expanse of the Americas, waiting to be conquered.

If a preening fop like Cortez could beat these proud savages, how much more could Francisco Pizarro achieve? Just like when he was a child, he imagined himself in front of the King. This time he was being celebrated, a parade of spoils behind him. Just like Cortez, he was granted status and wealth, but his was beyond even what his cousin had now gained. In the dream, Cortez watched as bitterly as Pizarro had just done, until Pizarro himself called him out of the crowd and ordered him to kiss his boot. With all the courtiers of Spain watching, and the King at Pizarro's back, Cortez bowed down and obeyed.

Pizarro let go of the knife handle and slid back through the crowd. His eyes sparkled as he dreamed of a far better revenge.

CHAPTER SIX

Cuzco

A fly was trapped in a cobweb above the Emperor's bed. Dying, it wriggled and kicked its legs, but its life's energy was all but gone. Those movements were the last, desperate twitches of something departing the world.

The cobweb had been there since Atahualpa returned to Cuzco three days before, responding to an urgent summons passed north by the empire's relay runners. His father was dying, struck down by the same unstoppable disease that had taken so many in the past two years. Supay, the god of death, hovered over him, accompanied by the demons that bore the god's name — invisible, silent, waiting to drag the Emperor to the inner world. Few servants dared go close to their ruler, and none would do so for something as trivial as sweeping away a spider's web.

Atahualpa reached out and grabbed the tangled fly, crushing it in the palm of his hand. As he stepped back he noticed Huascar looking up at him, one eyebrow raised. He was not going to get drawn into responding to that expression. Whatever his brother wanted to goad him into, he would keep his calm. He would not get drawn into the political games of court, any more than Huascar would trust him with a part in those games. Each of them had his own sphere, and both were glad at the expansion in the north, the chance for Atahualpa to live far from the heart of the empire.

For now, though, they were forced together.

The Emperor, divine guardian of the Incan Empire, opened his eyes, forced himself up onto his elbows, and pushed his body back against the cushions at the end of his bed. He was trembling, his skin pale except where the disease had marked it with patches of livid red. A servant changed the cooling bandage on his head and cast the old one, soaked with the divine sweat of the Emperor, into the fire.

"I am dying," the Emperor said.

"No, Father," Huascar said, and the assembled courtiers murmured their agreement.

Huayna Capac, Emperor of the Incas, looked at his silent younger son.

"Well?" he said.

"You will not live out the hour," Atahualpa said. As his father watched him he ceased his pacing, waiting for more words of command. Behind him, someone was whispering their shock at his response. He had no time for such people.

The Emperor laughed, the sound turning into a rasping cough. Huascar, glaring up at Atahualpa from his seat, handed the Emperor a cup of water.

"No." The Emperor waved the cup away. "Too late. Everything tastes of blood."

A pained look crossed his face. Sweat plastered his black hair to the sides of his face, yet there was still nobility in his features.

"I have decided the succession." At the Emperor's words, two scribes in simple brown tunics stepped forward. They held no instruments in their hands, but they would not need them. They would carry the words they heard directly to the rest of the court, and from there take them to be recorded. "I have spoken with Inti of the sun and Apu of the mountains. I have swallowed the coca leaf and followed my dreams to guidance. I have seen what must be. Huascar, you and Atahualpa will share my empire."

"What?" Both brothers spoke at once, though there was a very different tone to their shock. Atahualpa felt stunned that his father had even considered him for this. He deserved the whole empire, but he had thought that he was too blunt, too outspoken to have kept his father's favor, that success in war had not been enough to earn what passed for the Emperor's love. As for Huascar, everyone knew that he had expected to inherit, and his outrage at this turn of events was clear in his voice.

"Huascar, you are a great worker of men and manager of the court." Huayna Capac smiled at his son. "I am proud of the leader you have become and have every faith that you can govern. But you lack strength or courage in arms. Yours are the subtle, thoughtful arts, and you have no place at war.

"Atahualpa." The Emperor turned his gaze. "You have always been rough and disobedient. You lack the patience and discipline needed to maintain the law and to administer a state. But a fire burns in you that makes you a fine warrior — bold, strong, courageous. Your campaigns have seen our lands grow and torn up rebellion from the north by its roots. You bring order, control, and security. You will run the armies, keeping our empire safe. With each passing summer, it will grow larger and stronger beneath your might."

He sank back against the cushions, closed his eyes, and took two deep breaths. Then he opened his eyes again.

"You will learn to work together," he said. "Just as Manco Capac and Mama Ocllo together created the lands of the Inca, so will you two together make those lands grow. Under you, our nation will become greater than ever before, a power beyond any seen in the world. This is what I see for our people. This is what I leave to them."

Murmurs ran through the assembled courtiers. It seemed that Atahualpa was not the only one to be surprised at his elevation. Some smiled at him. More scowled.

"But, Father, this is unfair," Huascar leaned forward, cringing a little as he came close to his father's diseased body. There was softness in his voice that could not balance the grimace poorly hidden on his face. "Everyone knows that I am to be emperor. Such a division will be harmful to the empire. We will lose clarity of leadership. You risk everything you have built falling apart. Give the empire to me."

The Emperor shuddered as he turned his head.

"Do you say the same, Atahualpa?" he asked. "Are you too unwilling to share power?"

"No, Father." Atahualpa shifted from foot to foot. He would have been happier out on the frontier, sneaking through the jungle, climbing rock faces, hunting down enemies of the empire. But his father's will was his command. A soldier must bear discomforts for his cause, and so must a leader, even if that discomfort was as intense as working with Huascar. "Your wisdom shows in your words. Your will is mine. I will do you proud."

"Heh." Huayna Capac closed his eyes. "From anyone else, I would think you were being politic. But from you..."

His words drifted off into silence. His chest stopped its dramatic rising and falling. Atahualpa laid a hand on his father's chest and felt no heartbeat. Supay had taken him.

He looked across at his brother. They were emperors now.

CHAPTER SEVEN

Panama

Pizarro was sweating from head to foot. It drenched his tunic and hose, made his underclothes cling to him, and caused the plates of his armor to rub against his flesh at the joints. When he had seen Cortez a decade earlier, his cousin made a suit of armor look as easy to wear as a fine shirt. Years of campaigning had taught Pizarro otherwise, and months of trudging through the jungle had reinforced the point.

Ahead of him, Balboa and their native guide were fighting their way through a thicket of lush green undergrowth, the sort of rich plant life that would never have survived on the plains where Pizarro grew up. There were marvels in this new world, and they still lifted his heart as he thought of the riches they could conceal.

"When we find it, I'm going to test the waters with a swim," he said. "I'll strip off this glorious armor, and the ripe clothes beneath. It may be a hardship, but it's an explorer's duty to truly feel the things he discovers."

Beside him, Diego de Almagro grinned. The expression was distorted by the puckered skin emerging from the bandage wrapped around the upper right side of his face — where his eye had been. Pizarro wondered if the wound was entirely healed, and if his friend was hiding the results beneath the bandage. Whatever lay there, it was a terrible fate to have befallen a fine man. The squat, muscular Almagro had never been beautiful, but if the wound didn't heal correctly then he would be truly ugly.

"When we find it, I'm going to test the sands with a nap," Almagro said. "It'll be nothing like the luxury of sleeping upon rocks and tree roots for the past month. But if we are to claim this coast for the King of Spain, then I must provide him with a full report of all its horrors."

"When we find it, I'm going to-" Pizarro began the familiar rhythm, but their game was cut short by a shout from up ahead. In alarm, both men drew their swords and rushed after Balboa, who had disappeared from sight.

As they burst out of the undergrowth, they caught sight of their leader. He was on his knees, not at the hands of hostile savages, but with his hands raised in a prayer of gratitude at what lay before them.

It was a glorious sight. Past a beach of golden sand lay the vast blue expanse of the ocean. They had crossed the Americas. They had found the other ocean.

"God be praised!" Pizarro exclaimed.

"God and the King!" Almagro said.

They flung their arms around each other with a muffled clang of crashing armor plates. Both men burst out laughing as joy and relief flooded them.

As always, Pizarro was the first to emerge from joy and into hard practicalities, stepping back to assess the land around them.

A flag flapped in the breeze as one of the attendants unfurled the colors of the Kingdom of Spain.

"I claim this land and this sea in the name of the King of Spain." One of the priests had his Bible out and held it high as he intoned the words. "By order of His Majesty and under the rights granted to him by His Holiness the Pope. Long live the King, and may God bless us all."

A tear ran down the priest's cheek.

"Congratulations, sir." Pizarro strode over to Balboa and clapped him on the shoulder.

"Congratulations to you, too." Balboa stood and shook hands first with Pizarro and then with Almagro. "I could not have done it without you both. You shall have generous portions of the treasure we've gathered. We're rich, boys, rich!"

They laughed, gaining a stern look from the priest. But Pizarro was sure that God smiled upon them, even if his emissaries didn't. After all, they were bringing Christian civilization to this barbarous world.

"There's more to come," Balboa said. "I have every confidence that His Majesty will make me governor of Panama. After all, who knows this land better than I do? And when that happens, my lieutenants will have the world at their fingertips. Fine houses, slaves, luxuries, your share of taxes from the land. Everything you've dreamed of, boys. Everything I've heard you jabbering about around the campfire. It's yours now."

"We've earned it, Governor." Pizarro waved toward the jungle they had trudged through. "Now excuse me. I promised not ten minutes ago that I would test these waters for His Majesty."

"A man must keep his word," Balboa said, and turned to organize the attendants.

Taking Almagro by the elbow, Pizarro led him toward the edge of the ocean. The surf broke upon the sands in soft white crests, like lace that appeared then vanished back into the blue.

"I swore to sleep, not swim," Almagro said.

"Listen first." Pizarro looked back, checking that there was no one else in earshot. "We're not staying in Panama, not once we've been paid."

Almagro raised the eyebrow that could be seen. His bandage slipped, revealing a little of the torn flesh beneath.

"What about all those luxuries for the governor's lieutenants?" he asked. "The houses, the slaves, the plantations."

"Don't tell me that's enough for you," Pizarro said. "Playing Balboa's henchman."

"It would be enough for a while," Almagro said. "But you're right, not for long. Balboa's been good to us, but it's not the same as being my own man."

"My thoughts exactly," Pizarro said. "There's more wealth to be had, more power for those blessed by God and their own will, and more adventure along the way. I've heard that the greatest treasures are south of here, and I mean to launch my own expedition in search of them. I need a partner I can trust. You're coming with me."

He laid a hand on Almagro's shoulder and looked at his friend with his most serious expression. Almagro's one eye sparkled as if the gold he dreamed of lay glinting in its corner.

"I'm in," he said. "Once this expedition's done, you head back to Spain to raise the men. I'll get things organized at this end."

"To our new partnership." Pizarro stuck out his hand.

Almagro took it as if to shake, then pulled him close in a hearty hug.

"To our new partnership," he said. "And all the riches of the south."

CHAPTER EIGHT

Cuzco

Eight days was too long to stay unproductive. Atahualpa understood that his father's funeral was important. The mummification process and the presentation of offerings were all vital in ensuring that in death the late Emperor would look kindly upon those who succeeded him and that the power of the gods would pass from father to sons. Atahualpa proudly wore the gold needed as a conduit for his new divine power and followed the right rituals to ensure his father's passage to Ukhu Pacha — the inner world. But still, eight days was a long time.

He stood away from the burial chamber, looking down the hill at the palace. The royal residence was built of finer material than the burial mound. The stones were smoothly cut, the rooms were large and comfortable. The burial chamber, on the other hand, was rough and cramped, and Atahualpa could not stand another minute in there with Huascar and the elders. He was sure his father would not mind the disrespect. His final wishes had seen Atahualpa's many past failings forgiven; one more small transgression could hardly offend.

A fire burned on the hillside, despite the warmth and brightness of the day. Priests burned the things the late Emperor had left behind — his clothes, his plates, cuttings from his hair — as they had at the end of each year of his rule. Thus was the purity of Inti's descendant and messenger maintained.

Atahualpa walked toward the fire. It was a pleasing sight, an element of raw power turning all around to ash. Next year, it would be his leavings cast into the flames.

His and Huascar's.

Soft footsteps approached from the burial chamber. The servants were keeping their distance, and most of the other attendees preferred to stay away from Atahualpa's glowering. Only one person would talk with him now.

"Your lands are beautiful in this light." Cuyoc wore a black cloak over her white dress. Simple, well-made clothes, as befitted the eldest daughter of the Emperor at his funeral.

"This part will be Huascar's," Atahualpa said. "It is a place of politics, not war."

"All of it will be Huascar's if you aren't careful," Cuyoc said. She slid her arm through his and drew him away from the burial chamber. "The minute you left the elders conspired with him. They fear you."

"Let them," Atahualpa said. "These soft old men will never love me. Love is only one way to rule."

"Perhaps," Cuyoc said. "Or perhaps-"

"Brother," Huascar called out from the entrance to the burial chamber. "You should come. The elders wish to have words."

"That was too quick," Atahualpa said. "They have not had

time to plan my overthrow."

"Not unless they had already been scheming." Cuyoc looked up at him with concern. "Perhaps the lizards have been preparing for this day for a long time. Our brother's favor is the fatted swine on which they plan to feast."

Unhooking his arm from hers, Atahualpa walked toward the burial chamber. The elders stood blinking in the daylight, with Huascar in their midst. Around them, the servants drew closer. Atahualpa noticed that each servant was male, tall, and muscular. He was used to being around warriors; their presence never alarmed him.

Until now.

"Brother." He nodded to Huascar. "Elders. Share these words of yours."

One of the men stepped forward. Atahualpa wished he had paid more attention to their names, but he had been absent from court for too long and preoccupied with his father's illness since returning.

"We believe that your father's mind was not right in his final hours." The elder's eyes were almost as dark as his hair and black funeral robes. "This strange illness, it plays with a person's mind. Weakens it. Distances it from the wisdom of great Inti."

"Speak plainly," Atahualpa said. "I can see your intentions and have no desire for flowery tales. I am the heir to voice of the sun. Assume that I am no fool to be won over by your supposed reason, and get to the point we all know must come."

A pair of caracaras circled in the sky above them, their cries a lament for a body hidden away, stonewalls preventing them from feasting upon its flesh.

"Very well," the elder said. "Dividing the empire weakens it. We want one emperor."

"And you have chosen one."

"You are a warrior, Prince Atahualpa."

If the elder was nervous, then he hid it well. Atahualpa wondered if that was a matter of courage or if he didn't realize how easily Atahualpa could kill him. A twist of the neck and it would all be over. He was tempted, but kept his temper in check. A war leader had to control himself or lose everything.

"We do not need to be led by a warrior," the elder continued. "We need a statesman, someone to bring peace and stability."

"My father believed that I would bring territory, wealth, and glory," Atahualpa said. "Do you not want those?"

"You bring war. War brings risks. We have had enough of risk."

"You would ignore my father's dying wish?" Atahualpa clenched and unclenched his fist by his side. Control was becoming harder and harder to maintain. If he had come armed then this man would be dead already. To disrespect his father was one thing. To disagree with him even. But to disobey him? It would not stand.

"We will ignore that wish," the elder said. "All of us."

"And if I choose not to? If I stand true as stone?"

"Your brother feared you would say that."

The elder raised his hand and there was a flurry of movement as the servants leapt toward Atahualpa. He punched the first one as soon as he was within reach, sending him staggering back with blood pouring from his nose. A backward elbow sent the next to his knees, clutching at his injured throat. Atahualpa ducked beneath the arms of another man, kicked and punched as he tried to break clear of the mob. But he was one warrior, and they were many. Just as Cuyoc came in sight, standing a dozen feet away with a few other servants, he found himself dragged back into the heart of the fight, fists pummeling him.

"Now." The sharp clarity of Cuyoc's voice was unexpected.

The rhythm of the brawl shifted, and suddenly not so many men were punching Atahualpa. Blood spattered the back of his neck, and a hand gripped him tightly around the wrist, yanking him out of the melee. He raised his fist to strike his captor, and realized just in time that it was Cuyoc, a knife in her hand. Three servants with matching blades flanked her. Blood was dripping from their knives and running from wounds on the men who had tried to seize Atahualpa. Behind them stood the priests who had attended the fire, flaming brands raised.

"Quick." Cuyoc dragged him toward the road out of town. "We must be gone as swiftly as the wind, before they gather their courage and their weapons."

Atahualpa glanced once back over his shoulder. Huascar stood beyond the bloodied servants. There was no shock in his face. No surprise at the attack on his brother or the way it had ended. Only a grim determination, and an all too familiar hostility.

There would be no joint rule.

CHAPTER NINE

The Atlantic Ocean

Pizarro looked out from the bow of the ship at the endless expanse of the Atlantic Ocean. Ahead of them, to the west, was the New World. Soon he would be back, and praise be to God for that.

Had the journey felt the same to Columbus, he wondered, when that man sailed the ocean less than fifty years before? Had he felt the same sense of excitement Pizarro did at the prospect of new lands, wealth, and adventure? Or had his purpose, that mission to explore the Indies, given a different sensation to the great man? Had he felt determined, uncertain, wary, bold? Had the sea thrilled him as it did Pizarro? Had he dreamed of the lands he would reach? Or had his attention been swallowed up with the setbacks and minutiae, the hunger and sickness, rations and account books that plagued any great voyage?

Ropes creaked as the wind turned and the sails with it. The ships were moving faster than they had in the past week. He assumed that was a good sign, and not a prelude to a destructive storm. The weather reflected his eagerness to cross the ocean and set to work. But, could a storm, like a man, be overeager?

Pizarro liked to think that Columbus had been eager too, and as ragged as him by this point in the voyage. After all, Columbus too had spent months mustering men and supplies, seeking the resources he needed. There was little time or money to spare for costly clothes when every hour was time that could be spent recruiting, every gold coin the promise of armor or shot.

The ocean remained the same, no matter what men found on the far side. But, the men, they could be different.

"Lost in thought again, Francisco?" Hernando joined him at the rail, leaning forward as he looked out across the waves. The youngest of the Pizarro brothers retained an energy that had long since been worn out of Francisco, replaced with the grimmer determination of age. Even Hernando's face was the handsomest of them all, unravaged by time.

"Over that horizon is our fortune." Pizarro pointed into the distance. "Never again will the Pizarros return to the dust and poverty from that we were born."

"You should be a poet." Hernando grinned. "It's never too late to take up the arts."

Pizarro snorted. "Such fripperies are not for me. My art is war, war and the wealth it brings."

"Such a shame." Hernando shook his head. "You've seen a whole world of wonders, the very talk that makes my heart race, yet your soul trudges along the same dull path as Juan and Gonzalo."

He nodded back along the deck, to where their two brothers sat playing dice with some of the sailors; Gonzalo with a look of intense concentration that could have shut out the whole of the rest of the world. If Pizarro could turn even a fraction of that focus upon their goals, then he was certain his brothers would do him proud.

"How long until we reach Panama?" Hernando asked. "I long to see these golden beaches and emerald jungles."

"A week," Pizarro said. "Perhaps more. I have only made this voyage once each way before, and there are no signs I can judge the distance by. The captain would know better."

"I would rather talk with you." Hernando nodded at the game once more. "Our captain is as preoccupied as our brothers. You have been tight lipped since Barcelona, but do you think we have the men we need?"

Pizarro frowned. This was a question he had been avoiding addressing, even to himself. At the moment, he relied more on hope than on numbers. That had seen him through other expeditions, but those were not ones he had been running. With the wealth accumulated for over a decade in the balance, he could have done with more certainties.

"A hundred men and fifty horses." He sighed and stroked his beard, with its growing strands of grey. "Some with us now, others to follow later. It is not all I would have wanted, but it was all I could muster."

"We could have waited longer," Hernando said. "Let our crusade grow."

"The first recruits would have grown impatient," Pizarro said. "And Almagro is awaiting our return. He may have had more success than us."

"Will he recruit natives?" There was an edge of excitement in Hernando's voice. "Exotic warriors garbed in feathers and gems?"

"Certainly not," Pizarro said. "Men like us, but whose expeditions are over. Ones looking for new opportunities."

"Are there many of them waiting?"

"There had better be. If not then this may go to waste, and my wealth with it."

"Don't be so dour." Hernando nudged him and grinned. "You're a wealthy man, a modern Midas. Unless you've forgotten how you did that, we can do it again."

"How could I forget?" Pizarro thought of the jungle heat, the sweat soaking his skin, the insects biting at him, the bitter fights against natives. Then he thought of the gold he had taken from them, often jewelry ripped from their bodies in the moments after battle. The thoughts of wealth and excitement stirred him once again, and he smiled.

A shout made him turn. Juan's face was a picture of fury as he stared down at the dice. Gonzalo passed him a jug and he drank deeply, red wine dribbling down his chin. His expression shifting to a grin, he raised the jug in salute, first to his fellow gamblers and then to the lookout in the crow's nest.

"To the New World!" Juan yelled, and the other men cheered back.

Pizarro found himself grinning too. Like Columbus before him, he would carve his name into the memory of mankind. His brothers were around him, the future before him, and soon the world would be his.

CHAPTER TEN

The Andean Highlands

There were thousands of warriors on the plain below, a vast mass of men carrying spears and axes, clubs and shields. Slingers were along the flanks, already whirling their weapons around their heads as they tested the range to the tree line. There were twice as many men as Atahualpa had up here on the ridgeline with him.

The clouds parted and sunlight sparkled off a figure in the center of the army. Huascar still sat on his ceremonial litter, as he had for the whole journey from Cuzco. Atahualpa's scouts had delighted in that detail. They knew that their leader also had such a seat, but he would not ride it into war. Not when the men carrying it could instead have carried weapons. Not when their leader could instead have been fighting.

"Will you ask for terms of surrender?" Cuyoc asked. She looked no less elegant in the practical clothes of a warrior than she had in palace robes. Though she carried no weapon, the men accepted her among them — the sister and wise council of their emperor, the one true Emperor, usurped by the schemes of his half-brother.

"Certainly not," Atahualpa replied.

"We are outnumbered," Cuyoc said, "and that is not going to change."

"It does not matter." Atahualpa pointed down at the plateau and raised his voice. "Look at those men. Mercenaries brought out for pay. A few weeks ago they were in their soft, warm beds in Cuzco. And my men? We were in the north, fighting for the empire. Oh, we slept in Cuzco once. But we fought our way from there to the heart of the enemy, laying waste to all who stood before us. Do you think these slugs can stand against such men? I tell you all, they cannot. Any that survive will slink back to their soft, warm beds. By the end of this day, the empire will be ours."

The men around them cheered, the sound rippling out through the army, echoing from the mountains and across the lowlands below.

Cuyoc smiled and bowed her head. "Very wise, oh, Emperor."

Atahualpa returned the gesture.

"Now to war," he said, and turned to give orders to his officers.

Soon they were marching down the slope, through jungle that was less dense than the northern campaigns. One detachment of veterans broke off and headed to the left, another to the right. Hidden from the enemy by foliage, they would make their way around the open land in which Huascar's army was assembled.

Atahualpa led the rest of the army to the edge of the tree line. He saw the moment in which the enemy spotted them. Their lines formed up, facing toward him. A few sling stones rattled off the trees and thudded into the ground.

"Come out and fight!" one of the mercenaries yelled. "Or are you too afraid?"

Others joined in the shouting. Nothing they said moved Atahualpa. Though the fire of war burned in his soul, he held it back. Huascar could have stood in the center of that line exposing his bare buttocks, and Atahualpa would have waited patiently for his time to come.

Not that Huascar would ever risk himself in the front line. The campaign had already taught Atahualpa that much about his brother.

Half an hour passed. Huascar's lines crept slowly forward as the men, impatient for battle, taunted the warriors in the trees. A lack of discipline. At last their commanders gave up on waiting for Atahualpa. They had more men, and that made them confident. Rightly so — they outnumbered the forces still with Atahualpa four to one. If this went wrong, then he was doomed.

Drums beat at the back of the formation, and Huascar's men advanced. They wore fine headdresses that matched the red and blue tassels hanging from their shields. They looked bold and fearsome, but looks can deceive. Their headdresses were no match for the hearts of Atahualpa's men.

Step by step, the mercenaries came closer, their slow advance turning into a jog and then a charge, roaring as they streamed toward the tree line.

At last, when he could see the whites of their eyes, Atahualpa nodded to Cuyoc. She raised a horn to her lips and blew.

A long note rang out across the clearing. For a moment the world became still, Atahualpa frozen in one terrible moment of time as he waited to see if his planning had paid off.

Then came the responding shout.

Atahualpa's veteran detachments poured out of the trees to either side of Huascar's force. Racing forward, they closed the gap before the enemy could reorder their lines. There were screams of rage and pain as fighting broke out.

"Now!" Atahualpa yelled and charged out of the trees, his men all around him. An enemy lunged at him with a spear, but he didn't flinch. He battered it aside with his shield, swung his axe, and saw the man go down in a spray of blood.

Then he was in the center of the fighting and everything became a blur. Hacking, slashing, leaping. Blocking the blows of his enemies and raining twice as many down upon their heads. Danger meant nothing to him. There was only the glory of combat and the certainty of victory.

It seemed that only moments had passed before he stood in the middle of the field, panting and dripping with blood, watching his broken foe. Huascar and his guards had pulled back to the far edge of the plain and were retreating south. The rest of his men were scattered and broken. Some were fleeing into the jungle, only to be cut down by Atahualpa's men as they went. Others had thrown down their arms in surrender. A few fought on, small clusters of men surrounded on all sides by their enemies, showing courage to the bitter end. Atahualpa swore to himself that any of those they captured would receive the most merciful deaths.

Not like Huascar, fleeing in cowardice toward Cuzco. When this war was over, the traitor would meet a bitter fate.

CHAPTER ELEVEN

Tumbez, the Ecuadorian Coast

As they rounded the coast, Pizarro looked back at his expeditionary force. Seven boats, with nearly thirty men in each — double what he had brought with him from Spain. True, most of them were just young men, but the fire in their bellies made up for their lack of experience.

That fire was turning into impatience, for Pizarro as well as his men. All this time along the coast, and they had found nothing worth the taking. No signs of this supposed empire of the south, little more than a few fishing huts to keep them fed and entertained. Hernando, who stood grinning at the bow of the second boat, was still in fine spirits, enjoying the sights and sounds of the New World. But the rest were growing impatient, and Pizarro could not blame them.

They rounded a headland, men grunting at the oars, and Pizarro saw a sight to lift his spirits.

In many ways it was a town just like any on the Spanish coast. Boats in the harbor, trails of smoke rising from the cottages that filled its dirt streets. The walls of those houses were different from what he was used to — the stones rough and bare, the roofs steeply thatched. But a port was still a port, with all the promise it held.

There were walls around the town, and armed men standing along the quay. At long last: a challenge.

Turning to face the other boats, Pizarro raised his right hand. The captains of those boats, his three brothers among them, raised their right hands in understanding.

As they approached the quay, natives drew their boats closer to watch them. Children ran down onto the sands, while their mothers watched from doorways on the waterfront. There was something uncanny about the scene — an ordinary looking town surrounded by these strange, lush trees, inhabited by people with strange faces and stranger clothing. White cotton with colored trims stood out brightly against their nut-brown skin.

With a thud, Pizarro's boat hit a landing point and he stepped out, his interpreter beside him. In his hand was a sack.

Half a dozen men stood before him. They wore no armor, but the spears they pointed at the armored conquistador indicated that they were guards. They had that same straight black hair he had become so used to, and craggy features — all except the one on the end, who was portly and soft around the face, but with glittering piggy eyes. That one wore gold jewelry, and he was the one who spoke.

"They want to know why you are here," the interpreter said uncertainly. He was young, carried back to the Old World as a child, where he had learnt Spanish. Pizarro sometimes wondered if he had forgotten his own tongue in that time or was just too stupid to put the words together quickly.

"Tell them we have come to trade." Pizarro opened his

sack, displaying the cloth and candlesticks within. "Make them tell us what this place is."

The piggy guard leaned forward and said something in response to the interpreter. His eyes sparkled to match his gold as he looked into the bag. His companions eyed the Spaniards more nervously, hands clenched tight around their weapons.

Behind Pizarro, the men were climbing out of the boat. Others were mooring elsewhere at the docks or landing on the pale sands, their crews showing the guards sacks like the one Pizarro carried.

"He says this is Tumbez," the interpreter said. "He says that we should come up to the square. There are others there. Merchants, I think."

"Lead the way." Pizarro gestured up the hill, past the thatched buildings.

Piggy understood that one without translation. Soon they were ascending the rutted streets. Everyone came out to stare at them. Pizarro could only imagine what these people made of Christian warriors, with their pale skin turning red and their metal armor gleaming, like lobsters marching in the sun.

They reached an open space and Piggy stopped on the far side. Other men with spears had assembled there, fifty or sixty of them, some with that same acquisitive gleam in their eyes, others just looking baffled. Greed and stupidity — Pizarro lived for one and found himself constantly battling the other. He understood these men all too well.

The conquistadors assembled in front of the guards and waited.

It occurred to Pizarro that he could wait for Piggy and his

friends to push the situation and turn it into something bad. But why wait for an excuse? These people would grow to fear and hate him either way. The only justification that mattered was his backing from the King of Spain. With that, he could do whatever he wanted to these people.

He raised his left hand, while his right went to the hilt of his sword. Around him, his men dropped their sacks.

"Now," he shouted.

Two hundred blades rang as they were pulled from their scabbards. Some of the guards advanced toward them, their primitive spears at the ready. Piggy wasn't among them.

Juan was the first to attack. With a wild cry, he leapt at the nearest native — a woman carrying a basket of vegetables — and sliced through her neck. Blood fountained across his face as he turned upon the approaching guards, rosary stained red as it bounced off his breastplate. Gonzalo, a machine of calculated death, jumped to his side.

There were no intricate plans, no tactics beyond the simple things that all soldiers understood. Work together, pick off the weak, don't let yourselves become dispersed or surrounded. The square descended into bloody slaughter, and Pizarro felt his own pulse racing as he laid into the enemy, hacking to the left and to right, barely having to parry as blunt, soft-metal blades bounced off his armor.

Soon there were bodies everywhere and screams coming from nearby streets as half the boats' crew hunted down those who had fled.

"Stop!" Hernando strode out of the square, his voice full of frustration and his face wide with alarm. "Stop the slaughter. We've won."

Even the middle Pizarro brothers weren't listening to him — why would anyone else?

Francisco Pizarro stood at the end of the square, Piggy cowering before him. The fat guard commander had dropped his spear and was looking up at Pizarro in desperation. He pulled off his gold jewelry and held it up to the Spaniard, who snatched it from his hands.

"Interpreter!" Pizarro snapped, his temper still hot from battle.

"Yes, master Pizarro?" the trembling youth said.

"Tell them I want more of this." Pizarro held out the gold. "Any who want to be spared must bring it to me."

CHAPTER TWELVE

The Incan Empire

The ground was littered with bodies. Blood soaked into the soil, creating patches of thick, dark mud. Weapons lay where they had been abandoned. Those who followed the army were picking over the remains, gathering what was of value from the corpses as well as from the field. But they kept away from the Emperor, with his advisors and his trusted guards. The bloodstained Emperor with the fierce, victorious smile.

Atahualpa, undoubted ruler of the Incan Empire.

Across the field, a litter was carried toward him. Once, the greatest nobles in Huascar's retinue would have carried it. Now Atahualpa's soldiers carried it. The man who had ridden in it walked in front, his arms tied behind his back, his head hanging in defeat while he was nudged along by spear points.

"Kneel," Atahualpa commanded as his brother reached him.

Huascar sank to his knees. He did not look up.

"It's not fair," the defeated leader said. "I had more men. I am a better governor. The empire would have been safe with me."

"You are a greedy coward." Atahualpa spat upon his brother's head. There was blood in the saliva. He had been hit in the fighting and a tooth had come loose. "You took what was mine. Now I have taken it back, and your share with it."

The soldiers lowered the litter to the ground. Walking slowly around his brother, Atahualpa went to the seat. He ran his hand across the piles of blankets that made it comfortable despite its decorations of gold and precious stones. Setting aside his axe, he sat.

"This will suit me," he said, stroking the arm of the chair. "It is the seat of an emperor, after all. But in war, an emperor must stand. And he who loses must lie out for the vultures."

"Please, Atahualpa." Cuyoc stepped out of the group of commanders and looked her brother in the eye. There was no triumph in her face, only resignation. "There is no need to kill him. You have won, and he can still be of use."

"He defied the will of our father and the great god Inti," Atahualpa said. "Went against the word of the divine Emperor. That cannot go unpunished."

"He has been punished," Cuyoc said. "Humiliated for all the world to see. But our father's wish was that the two of you rule together, two halves of a single great mind, for the good of the Incan Empire. Would you, in your turn, defy that?"

"You wish us to rule together, after all this?" Atahualpa held out his hand, gesturing to the carnage scattered around them. "After his betrayal?"

"Yes."

"Please," Huascar said, his voice a hoarse croak. "I beg you."

"My sister is wise and cunning," Atahualpa said. "She understood what I needed when times were dark. But even the wisest of his subjects cannot match the understanding of an emperor. Great Inti granted me a vision of our future, and my brother has no part in it."

"Please." Cuyoc knelt in front of him. Blood seeped into her dress, but she ignored it. Overhead, the caracara circled. "Our nation has been torn apart in blood. More blood cannot reunite it, any more than an axe can heal the leg it has broken, but if you and Huascar stand together then you might present the bandage for our wounds."

Looking around, Atahualpa saw that more men were gathering. Some of them were nobles who had followed him, men who had gathered their war bands to his cause. They carried their weapons with pride. Others were men who had defied him, but who had survived the battle. Injured, dour faced, unarmed. They watched to see what he would do next, these men of influence. Men who had shown that they could lead, even if they could be led astray.

Were they what he needed in order to rebuild? And was Huascar what he needed to unite them around him?

He frowned. This was more like politics than he found comfortable. As he rested his head in his hand, he felt a pain — the tooth that had been loosened in the fight, grinding against his gums. The taste of blood filled his mouth like the bitterest salt water.

"Perhaps you are right," Atahualpa said. "Perhaps it would be easiest to unite our people with Huascar at my side."

Cuyoc smiled and bowed her head. "My brother is most-"

"Wait." Atahualpa held out his hand. "It is possible that you are right. But the moment my back is turned he will seize my place. Our empire cannot be united through treachery.

My brother has deceived me once. No man will ever trust him again."

He signaled to his guards. As Cuyoc's face fell in horror, one of them held his club out to the Emperor.

Atahualpa took the weapon and prepared to rise, to have the revenge he had wanted for so long. But as he did so he felt the arm of the litter beneath him — the seat of a politician, of an emperor in times of peace.

He handed back the club.

"Kill him," he said.

As his guards raised their weapons, Atahualpa sat back in his litter — the Emperor of all the Incas, appointed by gods and fate, watching his brother die.

CHAPTER THIRTEEN

East of Cajamarca, the Incan Empire

"It's amazing," Hernando said, turning in the saddle to look all around. "To think that a few days ago we were on the plains by the coast, and now..."

He waved a hand, taking in the mountains around them and the road leading uphill into the craggier peaks.

"I feel like Adam gazing upon Eden," he said.

Even Pizarro, who thought that he had become jaded of jungles and fine rocky outcrops, found himself impressed — not just with the scenery but also with the idea that someone had built a kingdom up here. He imagined the wealth they must have to achieve such a thing and smiled.

"Soon, all this will be ours," he said. "We will be governors of a new province, second only to the King in this part of his empire. Rich beyond dreaming."

"That's what I'm after." Gonzalo rubbed his hands together and nudged Juan. "Gold and women, not rocks and trees. I could have had those back in Spain."

Hernando sighed and shook his head while the other brothers grinned, the gleam of imagined gold bright in their eyes.

Birds circled in the sky overhead. Clouds rolled ominously in out of the west.

"An ill omen." Juan crossed himself and kissed the rosary hanging around his neck. Beside him, Gonzalo imitated the action. "Vultures and a storm."

"An ill omen, yes," Pizarro said. "But for those who stand against us. The birds arrive early to pick their carcasses clean."

This seemed to satisfy Gonzalo, but neither Juan nor Hernando looked comfortable at the words.

"Ride ahead," Pizarro said to Hernando. "Take a couple of men with you. Find out what the land is like. I think we may need shelter soon."

"Of course!" Hernando galloped off up the road, two of the other conquistadors close behind him.

Pizarro looked back down the trail. The men on foot were starting to lag behind. Not so much the slaves leading the baggage mules, but the soldiers in their armor, the young interpreters, and the friar with his bag full of sacraments. He regretted not resting them better after the last round of pillaging, when they'd seized that little village by the river, slaughtering the savages who held it and putting their families to flight. But he needed to press on.

Besides, this was what they had signed up for — hard work for good pay. No one had said this life would be easy. Life had never been easy for Francisco Pizarro.

They rode on for a while, until hoof beats came racing from the mountains ahead. He looked up to see Hernando galloping back down the slope.

"Francisco." His brother was out of breath, his eyes wild with something beyond excitement at the scenery. "You should come and see this."

Beside them, Juan crossed himself and settled a hand on his sword.

Setting the spurs to his horse, Pizarro followed Hernando up the track. There were things that alarmed his brother, including the blood lust shown by Juan and Gonzalo. But he had a sharp mind and a good eye. Away from the horrors of battle, Hernando's concerns were worth listening to.

His brother led him up the track, between stands of trees, and out onto a ridge. The armored riders who had accompanied Hernando waved at them from farther along the slope. There was urgency to their gestures, and when Pizarro reached them, he understood why.

Along the valley below them, an army was marching. Thousands of men striding forward in column. It was impossible to make out details, but no one travelled in such massive and disciplined formations except under arms.

"They outnumber us a hundred to one," Hernando said.

"More than that." Pizarro tried to count them, but there were too many, not all of them in sight.

"Is this how it felt to David when he first faced Goliath?" Hernando said, awe and tension mingling in his voice.

"I am no sandal-clad peasant." Looking around, Pizarro saw other figures closer by. A group of scouts in crude tunics watched them from a ridge. Two of them broke away and started running toward the army.

"Should we stop them?" Hernando reached for his sword — the lances were back with the baggage.

"No. It's too late to avoid being seen." Pizarro looked around. Below this ridge was a town, built in the same rough stone style as Tumbez had been. "Ride back and gather the men. We must prepare to face an army."

\#

The townspeople fled before most of the conquistadors even arrived. They looked in amazement at Pizarro and the two scout riders on their horses, then fled in terror as the armored men galloped toward them. By the time the infantry and baggage had arrived, every last doddering elder and mewling infant was gone.

There was a courtyard in the center of town. It was no fortified bastion, no castle that the small troop of Spaniards might defend, but as he looked at it, Pizarro fostered the beginnings of a plan.

The men bustled around him. Their movements were not frantic or chaotic, but focused and purposeful. They might not all be hardy veterans, but they had seen their share of adventure since arriving in the New World. They knew what they needed to do if violence was coming. The cavalry, with Juan at their head, collected their lances, checking the shafts for any damage in transit. Supervised by Gonzalo, the small number of harquebusiers loaded their weapons and attached match strings. Gonzalo lit a small oil lantern and shuttered it, keeping the flame alive for when it was needed to light the guns. A pair of cannons were unloaded from the mules and settled with much grunting and maneuvering into their frames.

"Over there." Pizarro pointed the cannon crews toward a building at the end of the courtyard with a shadowy overhang. "Get those cannons out of sight, but make sure they're ready to fire."

He turned to the harquebusiers.

"Into that building to the left. Keep the shutters closed until I give the word, or until things go to hell."

Gonzalo nodded and led his men away.

"Infantry," Pizarro continued, "Hernando will break you into groups and show you where to wait."

There was more movement and the thud of hurrying feet.

"Juan, take the cavalry to the right, behind those taller buildings. Stay mounted but keep your lances down. I don't want them to know that you're there. If surprise is all we have, then surprise is what we will give them.

"And someone find me the damned friar. His time has come."

CHAPTER FOURTEEN

West of Cajamarca

Riding high in his litter, Atahualpa looked down at the nobles, priests, and officials circling around him. Each one had some wisdom he wished to impress the Emperor with, some question to ask, some favor to beg. Some were wise, others pitiful, but all amused him with their eagerness to please. It was not like life in the north, all struggle and sweat. Here there was a different sort of strain, one that he barely felt and that he could only see in the faces of others.

His guards had the same look of disdain on their faces as him, though they did more to hide it. These courtiers, who expected reverence, were instead becoming a secret laughing stock to the army that had put all others to shame. The finest soldiers the Incan Empire had ever seen proudly surrounded him, their emperor as well as their general.

If this was politics, maybe he could get used to it after all.

A messenger ran up to the guards. They formed a perfect circle of armed men, keeping in step at ten yards away while Atahualpa continued his procession back to Cuzco, the entire army trailing behind him.

The messenger was soaked with sweat, a tunic clinging to

his body. He talked frantically with the guards, but Atahualpa could not hear him over the whining of the latest courtier.

"Enough," the Emperor silenced the courtier and turned to the messenger. "You, what is it?"

The messenger tried to bow and ended up stumbling backwards as the litter kept advancing toward him. Still he kept his gaze lowered in deference to the divine ruler.

"My Emperor," he said. "Tumbez has been destroyed."

The courtiers fell silent, even their whispered conversations abandoned at the news.

"Huascar haunts me from beyond the grave." Atahualpa clenched his hand around the arm of the litter. "Did he do this before his death or is it some remnant of his minions?"

"Neither, my Emperor." The man kept glancing over his shoulder, unwilling to turn away from the Emperor but worried about tripping on the uneven road. "Foreigners. Men from across the sea. They killed the people, took their gold, and burned the town."

"Cuyoc!" Atahualpa shouted.

"Here, my brother." She appeared as if by magic from amid the crowd of courtiers, leaving behind the subtle webs of intrigue through which she supported him.

"I do not know these southern lands so well," he said. "How quickly could we reach Tumbez with this army? There is more vengeance to be done."

A feeling like fire rose inside him, a rage he had thought slaked when he saw his brother die. First Huascar, now these barbarians. Everyone set on taking what was his. It would not stand.

"We would need tonight to reorder, prepare, and scout,"

Cuyoc said. "After that we could-"

"My Emperor." One of the guards approached, a man whose face Atahualpa recognized from campaign. A true veteran, and not a man to interrupt the Emperor lightly. "There is another messenger — one of the army's scouts."

This second messenger, his features weathered by years on campaign, hurried over at a wave of the Emperor's hand.

"My Emperor, a force of foreigners has been spotted to the east," he said, his gaze lowered and his backward pace steady. "They ride strange monsters and carry weapons that gleam like silver."

"The men from Tumbez," the first messenger said. "The survivors said that they carried weapons like this and that they lusted after gold as well as slaughter."

Atahualpa frowned.

"How many of them are there?" he asked.

"Less than two hundred," the scout said.

Curiosity mixed with anger in Atahualpa's mind. With new weapons, he could put even more of his enemies to flight. And what were these monsters that the strangers rode? Were they like the royal litter, a seat upon dozens of legs? Did they have wings like the caracara or claws like a jungle cat? There would be power in owning such beasts.

He would have to deal with these barbarian invaders, whether with war or with the threat of it. They would not be the first barbarians to bow their heads and accede to the power of the Incan Empire. Most of his warriors came from peoples who had made that choice not many generations past.

"I shall go to these foreigners," he said. "I wish to see what strange creatures Mama Qucha has cast from her divine waves onto my shores."

"My brother." Cuyoc reached up and laid her hand on his. "Why endanger yourself? Send some of these nobles to speak with them first, to find out what their business is."

"I am the divine vessel of Inti." Atahualpa shook off her hand. "I have just conquered an army of our own mighty nation. I have thousands of men behind me. I fear no band of savages."

"Marching the whole army up into the hills will take-"

"Camp them here." Atahualpa looked up the hillside, toward a town where the scout pointed. "I will take five hundred of my fiercest warriors, more than enough to face whatever we find there. One more adventure for the bravest of the brave."

The guards grinned at his words, and their commander started assembling the men. Up on his litter, Atahualpa smiled as well. His first encounter with foreigners as the unchallenged ruler of the Incas, and it was with strange men and their monstrous beasts. A glorious start to his rule, a sign of unimaginable glories to come.

He could get used to this business of politics.

CHAPTER FIFTEEN

Cajamarca

Atahualpa, Emperor of the Incas, looked down across the heads of his finest soldiers who filled the square of this small town from side to side. The men parted and his litter was brought forward, giving him a clearer view of the foreigners who stood before him.

There were two of them, and a young man who looked as though he came from one of the southern tribes. The boy looked terrified; his fingers so tightly interlaced that they turned almost white, and only he showed the deference due the divine Inca through his averted gaze. Beside him stood a man in a long grey dress, with thinning hair the same color. Around his neck he wore a piece of wooden jewelry, a necklace of round beads with a cross at the bottom. The cross had been cut badly, one limb left longer than the rest, spoiling its symmetry.

It was the third man to whom the Emperor's eyes were drawn. He looked as though he had been stretched out too long in the sun, his body long and thin, his skin pale and wrinkled as old cotton, most of his hair a faded grey. Stern, scarred features marked him out as a warrior, one who had survived many battles by the breadth of a llama's ear. He looked as though he had not shaved in years, his long beard a disgrace, hiding features Atahualpa could only assume were deformed or dishonest. Much of his body was covered in what looked like huge shells of a dull, silvery metal.

Atahualpa stifled a laugh. These men seemed to be led by an angry, old turtle.

The man in the dress stepped forward and began speaking in a loud voice. He was waving some sort of object in front of him, apparently a box bound in leather. Whatever he was saying, he treated it with the utmost seriousness.

As he reached the end of his speech, the younger man stepped forward.

"Greetings from King of Spain." The boy's Incan was halting and poorly accented, some of the words barely comprehensible. "Also his governor Francisco Pizarro. Your lands, part of Spain emperor are. Your gods no more — must follow one true god, be forgiven bad acts. Do as said, all be peace."

The boy nodded to the man in the dress, who stepped forwards and waved his box at the Emperor. A guard took it and handed it to Atahualpa. But while all of this was going on, the Emperor watched the third man, the one dressed in shells. There was hardness in his eyes, a look that never wavered.

Atahualpa opened the box. Except that it was not a box. It seemed to be a collection of strange rectangular leaves, bound together in leather, with wriggling lines all over them. That misshapen cross was on the cover.

What sort of gift was this for an emperor? And what was this nonsense, that there was only one god? Did he mean Inti or Apu, Con or Wiraqucha? Whichever god he spoke of, he risked the fury of the rest.

As for the idea that he, Atahualpa the triumphant, was ruled over by a king he had never heard of, he would soon answer that. Could they not see the gold that marked him out as messenger of the gods? Did they not recognize the divine Emperor?

He had had high hopes for these foreigners, whether as allies or opponents. Now he found that they were lunatics and fools.

Laughing, he tossed the strange box on the ground, to the clear horror of the man in the dress. So much for his grand moment of politics. He felt a fool, but there was no need to waste more time here.

Standing in his litter, he pointed a fist at the cold-eyed man — the one who was clearly in charge.

"The gods have graced me with victory, and I would not despoil it by fighting such as you," he said, and heard the boy starting to translate. "Return what you took from my town at the coast and leave these lands. If you do not, then I will crush you as I have all others who defy me."

∽

Pizarro listened as the translator mumbled the last few words into the silence now falling across the square.

Demands had not been enough. He had hoped that reason, and word of what Cortez had achieved, might persuade these savages into submission. Instead they showed open defiance and defiled the Holy Bible, its pages spread in the dust of the square.

He was outnumbered, but God was on his side. God and

his own ingenuity. That might just be enough.

"Friar, I suggest that you step back," Pizarro said. From the corner of his eye, he watched the translator hurry after the priest, into the shadows at the back of the square.

The so-called emperor was clearly growing impatient. At a wave of his hand, soldiers began to advance.

It was now or never.

"Fire!" Pizarro bellowed.

There was a moment of silence, in which he feared that his men had fled before the overwhelming numbers facing them. Then a roar filled the square as the cannons fired. Smoke billowed around Pizarro and Incan warriors went flying, their bodies smashed and twisted.

Shutters dropped from a building and the rattle of harquebus fire followed the roar of the cannons. More smoke drifted into the air and more men fell, one of them spinning on the spot as a bullet tore a bloody spray from his shoulder.

The litter tilted, several of its bearers among the dead. The Emperor tumbled to the ground.

"Now!" Pizarro yelled as the tension inside him gave way to exhilaration. Now came action. Now came the chance for glory.

Men rushed from the shadows and charged the bewildered Incas, sharpened steel slicing through them as if they were nothing more than water. Cavalry galloped in from the flank, and men screamed in terror at the sight of the beasts.

Pizarro had his own sword in his hand, fending off one attacker and then another. Part of him longed to leap into the fray, but he needed to follow what was going on around him.

The cavalry had reached the heart of the Incan lines. Two

of them grabbed the stunned Emperor and flung him across the back of a horse, then galloped off into the safety of the shadows at the side of the square.

"Finish them!" Pizarro laughed in excitement as the rest of his cavalry charged in, ten foot lances extended before them, skewering their opponents before trampling them in the dirt.

∼

Cuyoc watched in horror as warriors poured down the hillside toward her. The men who had been guarding her brother were in complete uproar, all courage and discipline lost. Few were even trying to fight, their weapons cast aside as they ran.

"Magic!" one of the men screamed. "The foreigners wield dark magic!"

A familiar figure ran toward her, one of the nobles who had borne Atahualpa's litter. Cuyoc grabbed him by the arms and forced him to face her.

"What happened?" she demanded. When the man didn't answer she slapped him across the face and his eyes grew even wider.

"Supay!" he exclaimed, his voice trembling as he spoke of the demons of the inner world. "They have Supay on their side, and when they roar it brings smoke and death."

Tearing himself from her grasp, he ran down the hill.

Cuyoc stared around her in bewilderment. How could this be happening, the greatest warriors of the empire turned into gibbering children?

More men ran down the hillside. Behind them came

monstrous beasts, the earth rumbling beneath their feet, men riding on their backs. These men carried long spears before them or hacked about with narrow swords that gleamed like clear rivers.

Hitching up her robes, Cuyoc joined the throng running down the hill. While her mind spun at the strangeness of it all, she ran not in fear but in determination — toward the safety of the main army, and the chance to prepare for whatever came next.

~

As the smoke cleared, Francisco Pizarro found himself standing in the middle of the square. All around were the dead and the dying, none of them his own. The royal litter lay on one side, abandoned in the trample of flight. Gold jewelry gleamed on the bodies of its bearers, and Pizarro eyed it greedily.

But it was not gold that had brought him this victory, even if gold would be his reward.

He stooped and picked up the Bible, now trampled and stained, out of a pool of blood. He turned it over, and found it open to one of his favorite passages.

"'When you go out to battle against your enemies and see horses and chariots and people more numerous than you,'" he read. Blood obscured the following lines but he continued, the words long learnt by heart. "'Do not be afraid of them; for the Lord your God, who brought you up from the land of Egypt, is with you.'"

He smiled, wiping away as much as he could of the blood, and looked around for the friar. The holy man was emerging tentatively into the square, rosary clasped in white knuckled hands.

"This day could not have gone better," Pizarro said, trying not to let his pride show before God almighty and his representative on earth.

"Praise be to the Lord," the friar said, taking the Bible.

"And to the King of Spain," Pizarro said. "Now let us count the gold with which they have blessed us."

PART TWO

CHAPTER SIXTEEN

Cajamarca

The sunset glowed red, the sky stained to match the earth. Pizarro sat on a rock at the entrance to the town, watching the valley below. The Incan army bustled like an overturned ants' nest, chaotic and bewildered. He was safe for the night.

Or so he prayed.

"We've finished moving the bodies," Hernando said, sinking wearily onto the ground beside him. "The town's clear if we have to fight again, though I pray we don't have to — my sword has drunk its fill of blood today."

Squinting across the valley, Pizarro tried to judge what was happening at the far side. Was that commotion more troops arriving? Were they mustering to depart? For all he knew they were preparing some dark ritual to their savage gods, marking their losses that day. Some cultures didn't need a body to conduct funerary rites.

"Even Juan and Gonzalo helped," Hernando said. "Mostly so that they could take the jewelry off the bodies, but even carrion can be helpful."

He nudged Pizarro, who continued watching the valley. Torches had been lit in a broad circle. That seemed more likely to be a service than troops preparing to march. Or perhaps a mustering of officers, to announce their plans and prepare an attack. He should have the guns repositioned so that they were facing down the hill.

For all the good that would do, it was a short-term solution. He had decapitated an empire, but he could not become its head with less than two hundred men at his back. As the thrill of triumph receded with the heat of the day, he had to face the cold reality that they were now at war, and vastly outnumbered.

"Francisco?" Hernando nudged him again, his elbow bouncing off Pizarro's breastplate. "Are you listening?"

"We can't do this by pure force," Pizarro said. "We've spent the element of surprise, and that was the most powerful weapon in our arsenal."

"So what now?" Hernando asked. "Retreat? Negotiate?"

"Something like that." Pizarro ran his fingers through his beard. Clots of dried blood fell into his lap. "Tell me your thoughts."

"Me?" Hernando asked in amazement. "I've never done anything like this before."

"Neither had I when I began," Pizarro said. "And you are at least as smart as I am, though you waste it on fancy words. So I say again, your thoughts."

Hernando took a long breath, his own gaze now on the valley below. A growing number of tiny figures assembled in that distant circle of torches.

"It is traditional to ransom captive nobles," he said. "The English once ransomed two kings at once, and thought themselves to be doing well, but an emperor would be worth a fortune. And as long as we threaten him, they have reason to keep the peace."

"That has potential." Pizarro nodded. He could feel an idea unfolding in the back of his mind, an adaptation of what Hernando had suggested. "But I think we can get more than treasure from this."

"The men will be disappointed," Hernando said. "They are much enamored of the wealth they have found here."

"Don't worry," Pizarro said. "You saw the jewelry we took from the battlefield. Imagine how much more there must be in their cities. There will be gold enough for everyone. But I think we can get more than that out of this man."

~

"They want what?" Atahualpa stared across the empty room at the boy who translated for the foreigners. His captives had removed all the furniture, and so he crouched on bare stones, his back against the wall, ready to spring into action should he need to. He had been caught unaware once already today and burned with shame at the thought of it. He would not be ambushed again.

But he could still be surprised.

"Gold," the boy said, pointing at the ear plug that the lean, grey foreigner held in his hand. Another one stood behind them in the doorway, younger than the leader but with similarly narrow features, a thoughtful expression on his face. It was an expression that reminded Atahualpa of Cuyoc during her less calculating moments. He prayed silently to Inti that his sister was well and not in the hands of these savages.

"Are they all holy men?" Atahualpa said.

The boy frowned for a moment, then realization crossed his face. It was a shift that was becoming all too familiar, as the boy struggled to understand and convey Atahualpa's words in the invaders' slithering tongue.

"Not for priest." The boy still pointed at the gold. "For be good. For...trade?"

Atahualpa paused, repressing the frustration that burned inside him, as much at himself as at the boy and his masters. What good was gold for trade? It would just end up in the hands of the holy eventually, and those who abused it would face the wrath of the gods. There was no point trying to buy or sell it.

Perhaps the boy had mistranslated. Perhaps these people were every bit as savage as their actions had shown. Whatever was happening, he needed to respond. He had failed enough today. Though he was still reeling from the shock of everything he had seen, he needed to pull himself together. He was a warrior, not some timid peasant farmer. He had seen slaughter on battlefields, had put his own brother to death. He could face this.

Mustering his strength, he forced himself to his feet, only then realizing how reluctant his mind was to let him leave his safe spot, across the room from foes who brought monsters and thunder to the battlefield. What fresh cowardice was this? He was the divine Emperor.

In three long strides he crossed the room. Fighting to keep his finger from shaking, he pointed at the gold in the grey man's hand and looked him in the eye. Then he spread his arms to indicate a great mass of gold.

The foreigner nodded slowly.

Atahualpa stepped back and looked around. It was a moderate sized, high-ceilinged room, one that could have feasted his family and a few guards. Stones lay heaped in one corner. He picked one up, reached as high as he could and scratched a line on the wall.

"Tell them that if they free me, I will fill this room with gold up to that mark," he said, his eyes meeting those of the grey man.

The boy translated. After a moment the grey man spoke, his voice hard and flat.

"He say gold first," the boy said, glancing nervously between the emperor and the conqueror. "Then go."

"I cannot gather the gold while I am locked up in here." Atahualpa dropped the stone. It clattered on the ground as he shrugged. "For that I have to run my empire."

Again the boy translated. As he finished, the smallest hint of a smile appeared at the corner of the grey man's mouth. He shook his head and spoke.

"Run empire from here," the boy said. "When gold here..."

He turned a questioning look on the grey man, who pointed to the line on the wall and then gestured toward the door, as if showing a guest out.

Reluctantly, Atahualpa nodded. What choice did he have? The grey man held everything of value here, including Atahualpa himself. What was a pile of gold compared with the life of a god emperor?

As he watched the men leave, he felt the fire of his soul dwindling to an ember.

CHAPTER SEVENTEEN

Cajamarca Town Square

"Did Mother ever tell you about the bull that shits gold?" Gonzalo asked. He turned as he watched the latest group of visitors cross the square, Spanish guards flanking them all the way through town. There were half a dozen men, all in loose white tunics decorated with blocky patterns in red and blue. One had gold jewelry in his ears and around his neck. He was probably a noble come to talk with the Emperor, the others his attendants.

"I didn't spend much time with Mother." Pizarro pictured a Trujillo backstreet and remembered the feel of a loaf of bread in his hands. Whatever feasts he attended, no food would ever be ingrained in his memory as well as that single loaf.

"You didn't miss out on much," Gonzalo said, apparently oblivious to the edge in his brother's voice. "Anyway, in this story there's a bull that shits gold. Makes some dumb peasant rich. That's what this lot remind me of — a glorious stream of gleaming, stinking shit worth more than everything I've ever owned in my life."

Pizarro clenched and unclenched his hand around the

sword hilt at his hip. His brothers were a valuable asset, strong men bound to him by blood and greed. They could even be good company, in the right moment. But this was not the right moment, and Gonzalo was certainly not the right brother for his mood. Not until they were ready to celebrate or to fight again.

"What do you want?" Pizarro asked.

"Who says I want anything?" Gonzalo placed a hand on his chest. "I'm your brother, can't we just-"

"Juan broached our last cask of wine half an hour ago," Pizarro said. "If you're not with him then you want something."

"Once again, you remind me why you're the leader." Gonzalo grinned. "All right, I admit there is something. When are we going to start doing this lot like we did the first lot, so we can gather up their gold?"

Spinning on the spot, Pizarro shoved his brother up against the wall of a crude stone hut, his arm pressed against Gonzalo's throat.

"Are you insane?" he hissed. "If we kill these people, their whole army could turn on us."

"But we beat them!" Gonzalo said, his face going red. "What's the problem?"

"The problem is that talk like yours could ruin everything." Pizarro took a step back, letting Gonzalo find his feet again. "Atahualpa has told his generals not to attack us, and they're doing as they're told. But what would you be thinking if you were down there, stewing on a defeat? Would you just accept it, or would you be looking for an excuse to fight?"

"I..." Gonzalo looked around at the dozen of their own

men scattered around the town square, all diligently looking away from the argument between their leaders. "I didn't think of that."

"Of course you didn't. And did you think about what will happen to the other gold they've started to deliver, if we grab these few passing through and rip away their trinkets?"

"Trinkets?" Gonzalo pointed at the half dozen Incas emerging from the Ransom Room. "That lot alone is carrying-"

"Enough." Pizarro held up a hand. "Do you remember how your golden shit bull story ends?"

Gonzalo shrugged. "Stopped listening. Stories always bored me."

"The man kills the bull," Pizarro said.

"I thought you didn't know it."

"Well I do. And what I remember isn't that stream of golden shit. It's the moment when the man gets hungry and too impatient to wait for the butcher to bring him a steak. He kills the bull, and he eats well, but all his gold turns back to shit. Do you understand what I'm saying?"

"Don't shit on your steak?" Gonzalo shrugged. "I don't know. It's just a stupid story."

Pizarro rubbed his temples. He really wasn't talking to the right brother for this.

"The point is that these people are our bull." He pointed at the Incas as they headed down the hill. "The gold they wear is the steak. And this whole empire, all its wealth and power, is the gold you would lose for the sake of that single meal. Got it now?"

Gonzalo nodded, eyes wide and grinning.

"There's more to that story than you'd think, isn't there?" Gonzalo said. "And you know what? I'm going to go see if I can get us both a steak. Those bloody llamas have got to be good for something — let's find out what they taste like."

He slapped Pizarro on the arm and walked away.

Pizarro looked around. The shadows were growing long as dusk approached. Atahualpa wouldn't have any more visitors today. None of the Incas ever came up here at night — Pizarro suspected they were too superstitious about the horses and guns to risk it. It might be time for him to visit and get the measure of where things lay.

Crossing the square, he pushed aside the curtain at the door of the hut they'd taken to calling the Ransom Room. In one corner, a small pile of gold glittered in the light coming through the windows. Next to it sat Atahualpa and Hernando, with the interpreter hovering nearby. A straw mattress and blankets were piled up in another corner, along with the remains of a meal as good as that the Spaniards themselves had eaten. As long as Atahualpa cooperated, they would keep him happy and comfortable.

"How was today?" Pizarro asked.

"Much the same," Hernando said. "I don't think they're sending up the top people yet, but each day there's someone a little more distinguished and covered in gold."

"Nothing that made you suspect they're planning an attack?"

"I haven't learnt many words yet, but no," Hernando said. "Not unless they're very nervous planners."

"Good." Pizarro turned to face Atahualpa, signaling to the translator as he did so. "Now let's learn more about our new empire."

CHAPTER EIGHTEEN

The Captives' Quarters, Cajamarca

The sun streamed in through the doorway, stirring Cuyoc from a restless night's sleep. It was hard to relax here, surrounded by barbarians, far from the comfort of Cuzco or the support of the court. True, half the court spent half their time plotting to undermine her influence so they could whisper their own words into her brother's ear. But at least that sort of scheming was familiar. These Spaniards were another matter entirely.

She pulled on her tunic and emerged from beneath her blankets. Atahualpa was already up, dressed in only a loincloth, doing stretches in the middle of the room. His movements were stiffer and less confident than usual, and a frown filled his face. Their two servants were outside the doorway, preparing food over a small fire.

"I'm going to ask for cushions," Cuyoc said. "And some furniture. You're the emperor, and your residence should reflect that."

"It could be worse," he said, lunging forward with one leg and then the other. "We could still be in the Ransom Room."

"If we were, we would be sleeping on gold by now," Cuyoc

said. "I prefer cushions."

One of the servants approached the Emperor, head bowed, a steaming bowl held out before him. The other servant passed a bowl to Cuyoc. It was a stew made of one of the region's sweeter varieties of potatoes — not bad, given the circumstances, but not everything she had hoped for with the civil war over.

"I could do you more good if I was with the rest of the nobility," she said. "You know they'll be scheming against you by now. With Huascar gone and you here, they'll be wondering if they can make a puppet of one of our brothers, maybe Manco. He's old enough to rule but young enough for them to bend him to their will."

Atahualpa sat down and stared at his stew.

"I need someone here whose judgment I can rely on," he said. "I trust these strangers to keep their word — after all, they are getting what they want from me. But they still need to be managed."

"Managed?" Cuyoc set her bowl aside and sat in front of her brother, looking him straight in the eye. "Brother, you cannot manage what you cannot control, and you cannot control these people any more than you can control great Inti."

"I do not need to control Inti to gain from his presence," Atahualpa said.

"But you need to trust him, and you cannot trust these Spaniards." The word "Spaniard" was a strange one to say, like all those she had learnt so far from these people. "They will not release you once their Ransom Room is full. Why would they, when they hold an empire in their hands?"

"What else can they do? They are a handful of men, and I the head of a mighty nation."

"Then resist them! You don't have to accept this."

A strange look danced briefly in her brother's eyes, something both wild and broken.

"They have tamed the thunder," he said. "They ride monsters. I am in no place to resist that. Not yet."

Cuyoc stood. She could not bear to be around Atahualpa when a gloom descended upon him like this. Seeing this broken man stare out through the eyes of her strong, decisive brother was too much to bear.

"I am going to see how the gold grows," she said, heading toward the doorway. "If that is your best hope, then we must know how it progresses."

Outside, half a dozen Spaniards stood in the dirt street, their breastplates gleaming in the sunlight. Their hands went to their swords as she emerged, and they watched her like eagles as she walked proudly through them. Passing the houses around the square, she could hear one of the men following her with lumbering footsteps, like an unshaped rock tumbling down a valley side.

There were more of them in the square, of course, guarding their precious house full of desecrated gold. The way they looked at her sickened Cuyoc — some lascivious, others with a darker hunger. Gritting her teeth, she strode past them, only to stop in her tracks as a tall figure emerged from the darkness of the Ransom Room.

Hernando Pizarro stopped too, a smile spreading across his neatly bearded face. It was not an unappealing face, for a Spaniard, a fact all the more remarkable for the similarity he bore to his sternly grizzled brother. Unlike his comrades, he did not stare at her with open greed or contempt, and though he did not look away as a barbarian should in the face of royalty, he at least offered her a small bow.

"Cuyoc well?" he asked.

It took her a moment to recognize the words, mangled as they were by his foreign accent. Hiding her surprise at his use of her language, she nodded.

"I am well," she replied. If he was intent on ingratiating himself — intent enough to learn to speak her language — then maybe she could find a use for this one, a way to learn about and manipulate their captors. "And you, Hernando? How does Inti's first light find you?"

He opened his mouth, hesitated, and then shut it. He looked up as he grappled with something in his mind, and then turned his gaze on her again.

"I not much word," he said, making a small gesture with his hands. "You more word me?"

Despite herself, Cuyoc laughed.

"Yes, I will teach you more," she said. "Your translator is clearly as capable of the task as a fish is of flying."

Hernando said something in Spanish, and then they stood in awkward incomprehension, looking at each other. Finally, Cuyoc cut through the moment, gesturing past him into the Ransom Room.

"I want to look in there," she said, unsure if he understood a single word. "It seems as good a place as any to start teaching you."

Hernando spoke Spanish again and stepped aside to let her in. As the words slid past, it occurred to Cuyoc that maybe she could learn from Hernando, as well as he from her. Of all the Spaniards, he seemed the one with the greatest sense of honor, the one she could trust to teach her. And if she could do it without the other Spaniards noticing, or without them realizing how much she understood, then they might let information slip around her.

As she walked into the room, Hernando waited outside, apparently not having understood her invitation. Looking back, she waved him in. Then she turned toward the shining pile in the corner of the room.

"Gold," she said pointing toward it.

"Gold," Hernando repeated.

"Good," Cuyoc said. "Now you."

She gestured from the Spaniard to the treasure. He smiled and said a word in his own language. Cuyoc repeated it, apparently not well, as he made her do it twice more before nodding his approval.

She smiled back at him, pride and calculation mingling in her heart. She knew her first word of Spanish, and it was the word at the heart of all their dealings. She knew the word for gold.

CHAPTER NINETEEN

Cajamarca

There were more soldiers in the valley than there had been the day before. Hernando watched them from the hillside. It was almost beautiful to see the patterns of movement as nobles and their entourages moved around that distant camp, tiny dots in bright white, red, and blue, sometimes shining as the sunlight glinted off their jewelry. He felt like a magpie, looking out for the most precious treasure to snatch away.

"Hernando?"

The voice by his ear made him jump. Heart thudding, he turned to see Cuyoc, a mischievous smile on her face as she sat down beside him, straightening her robes.

"How do you do that?" he asked.

She turned her hands palm up, their sign for "I don't understand." While the words he had used were small, they had an abstract quality that made them harder to explain. Most of what they each knew of the other's language came in the form of nouns and verbs, clear things that they could point to or demonstrate.

"Never mind," he said, and received the same response. Searching for a topic of conversation, he pointed at the latest group of Incas coming up the hill, under the watchful gaze of the Spanish guards. They were led by a youth in his teens, whose jewelry and stiff-backed entourage marked him out as someone of note, in contrast with the nervous innocence of his face.

"Who is that?" he asked.

Whether or not Cuyoc understood the words, she got the question.

"Manco," she replied. "Brother."

"Your brother?" Hernando pointed at her and then back into Cajamarca. "Atahualpa's brother?"

She nodded. "I brother."

"My brother," he said, emphasizing the first word.

"My brother," she repeated.

"Your brother." Hernando nodded, and they both smiled.

∽

The dining table was a rickety affair — long planks laid across barrels in one of the more substantial houses, flanked by more planks on more barrels for seating. Hardly a governor's court, but enough to add a layer of civility to the evening meals of the expedition's commanders — the Pizarro brothers, Almagro's lieutenant Hernando DeSoto, and the Friar Vicente. The meals were improving since the Incas had started bringing supplies up for their emperor, but the local tubers were no substitute for honest bread and meat.

"We've all spent time around Atahualpa." Francisco Pizarro looked down the dining table, eyeing his companions in the candlelight. "We've all seen what sort of man he is. Tell me about the others."

"Manco seems honest enough," the friar said. "And more amenable to new ideas than the rest. He has taken an interest in the Bible I showed him."

"An interest in its contents, or the idea of a book?" Pizarro asked.

"I..." The friar hesitated.

"What the good father is trying to tell us is that he has no clue," Gonzalo said. "He just wants to remind us all to be good Christian boys or risk divine wrath. Isn't that right, Father?"

"Don't disrespect the priest." Juan glared as he crossed himself.

"Or what, you'll deliver the hellfire yourself?" Gonzalo said.

"Or I'll show you what happens to those who bring bad luck down on others." Juan was on his feet, gravy dripping from the knife he pointed at his brother.

"Oh really?" Gonzalo stood. "Let me show you what-"

"Enough." Pizarro slammed his fist against the table, bringing silence to the room. Beneath the weight of his glare, Juan and Gonzalo both sat back down, though they kept eyeing each other. "Tell me something real."

"Ask Hernando," Juan said. "He's the one sticking it to the princess."

All eyes turned to the youngest of the Pizarro brothers. He kept his own gaze averted, focusing on the bowl in front of him.

"Tell me," Pizarro said.

"We talk," Hernando said, finally looking up at his brother. "Pleasant company is hard to get around here."

"Did he just-" Juan fell silent as Pizarro held up a hand.

"These people are savages," he said. "Not friends."

"I know, Francisco." Hernando sighed and pushed his bowl away. "But we need to learn about them if we're to keep them under control."

Pizarro didn't like the way his brother looked away, or the sadness in his voice.

"I want to trust you, Hernando," he said. "But I can't have you being won over by a mound of breasts."

"You have nothing to worry about," Hernando said. "I'm just trying to understand our enemy."

It was only words, and words could lie. But if Pizarro could trust anyone it was his youngest brother, the one who had always been honest, calm, and loyal.

"We don't need to worry about a princess," Francisco said. "What has anyone learned about their generals?"

∼

"What are you doing, spending all your time with that barbarian?" Atahualpa stared across the fire at his sister. It was not a cold night, but they needed the flames to perform ceremonies to Inti. If there was ever a time to call upon the god's favor, this was it.

And so here they were, in the street outside his prison house, standing around a pile of charred sticks and a sacrificial bird. The Spanish guards stared with open suspicion at their pitiful ceremony.

"If you would prefer for me to be among our people, then send me back to court," Cuyoc replied. "If not, let me do here what I do there — learn about your enemies and turn aside their schemes."

"It is one thing for you to do this at court," Atahualpa said. "Another to wander alone with a man whose blood is below that of peasants."

"A man whose brother has you captive," Cuyoc said. "Would you have me give up my best chance of freeing you?"

"Don't talk to me like I am one more fool caught in your web of schemes," the Emperor said. "I have seen the way you look at him; the way you hold yourself around him."

"I am not a little girl, susceptible to the winds of whimsy and a flattering face," she said. "I helped you master an empire, and right now I am the best ally you have. Treat me with the respect I have earned."

She froze, finger pointing at Atahualpa, a look of shock on her face. He realized that she was having the same thought as him — he was the emperor, the chosen of Inti, and she was just a woman. He could have her put to death for this disrespect. Other emperors would have. Should he now, to maintain his authority? And how could that be done, when he was a captive here?

"I am sorry, my Emperor." She looked away.

"As am I." Atahualpa felt his heart sliding into the darkness that engulfed his empire. He needed to hang on to something of the light. "My sister."

CHAPTER TWENTY

Cajamarca Town Square

Three litters sat in the middle of the square. None were as grand as the one on which Atahualpa had entered several weeks before, and which Pizarro now kept among the prizes he had taken. But each was still impressive, with a high-backed chair covered with soft blankets and a dozen porters ready to carry its passenger down the long road to Cuzco. A pair of grandly dressed Incas stood near the litters, one glaring at the Spaniards, the other toying nervously with the gold disk in his ear. When Pizarro stared at them they looked away.

Juan and Gonzalo stood with him at one end of the square, hands on the hilts of their swords, eyes roaming the area. They might not always be good company, but those two were always handy for a fight. At the other end of the square, a group of Incan warriors stood, axes and shields in hand, feathers protruding from their bronze helmets. They held themselves as proudly as any elite guard. The Spaniards watched them from every side, steel blades at the ready, matchlocks smoldering on harquebuses, ready to fire if trouble broke out.

The Incan warriors stared back at the pale-faced invaders,

their expressions as angry as any Pizarro had seen. The atmosphere was tense, and he didn't like it. It was all too easy for such situations to erupt into violence. But he was willing to risk it for what would come next.

"One of us should go with them," Gonzalo said. "This expedition is run by a Pizarro; the important parts should be overseen by a Pizarro."

"And there'll be women at this city," Juan said. "Maybe wine. I need a drink and a woman. My balls are swollen like a Frenchman's head."

Gonzalo glared at his brother, but it was too late for subtlety. Besides, Pizarro had seen through their pleas from the start. These two were as concerned with good oversight as he was with what they left in the latrine each morning.

"Almagro may not be here, but he is as much a leader of this expedition as I am," Pizarro said. The more he said it, the more he hoped others would take him at his word. He needed the extra troops Almagro was recruiting, and that meant he needed Almagro to consider himself an equal partner. For now, at least. "DeSoto is his man here. He's more than capable of overseeing this."

"Always the Hernandos, sticking themselves in where the rest of us should be," Juan said.

"Enough," Pizarro snapped. "I want you two pricks here, where I have your blades by my side, and where I can keep an eye on you. If I let you out of my sight you'll grope and kill everything between here and the coast, not always in that order. Let me tell you, it's hard to get cooperation from men whose wives you've taken, harder yet to squeeze gold out of the dead. But you two are just so stupid you might try. You wanted to know why you're not going to Cuzco? There it is. Now go, before I regret ever finding my family."

Grumbling to themselves, the two skulked away, seeking a corner to complain in. As a way to deal with dissent, it wasn't perfect. For all the gold slowly piling up in the Ransom Room, the men were growing tense, stuck in this town with nothing to do but wait and moan. Sleeping crammed together in tiny, stinking rooms for the sake of security, eating strange food that sometimes had to be tightly rationed. Half of them were struggling with stomach pains and diarrhea, all of them suffering from the stench. On top of that there was the native army, still many times their size, waiting just outside of town. No, sending troublemakers off to moan in a corner wasn't perfect, but until something changed it would have to do.

As Juan and Gonzalo departed, three other figures emerged from a nearby house. Clad in a breastplate, ridged helmet, and worn hose, Hernando DeSoto led the way. The satisfied smile he cast across the litters seemed out of place beneath his large, crooked nose and sunken eyes. Accompanying him were a grizzled ex-sailor and the expedition's notary, Juan Zárate, both armed and armored. Clerks who joined expeditions to the New World had to be as handy with the sword as with the pen — there was no place for idle hands when the fighting began.

"We're ready, master Pizarro," DeSoto said with a small bow. The others followed his lead.

"And your timing is perfect," Pizarro said, putting on a smile. The goodwill of Almagro's henchman was as important to his plans as Atahualpa's obedience. "This is an important mission, but I have every faith in your abilities."

"You honor me," DeSoto said, his tone indicating that it was the least he deserved.

"You honor me by accepting this task," Pizarro said. "I need a good pair of eyes and a sharp mind to assess whatever you find."

"You can count on me." DeSoto bowed a little more deeply.

"Save that until I'm a lord," Pizarro said. "Until we're all lords, and rich with the gold you're going to fetch."

"Very well." DeSoto straightened. "Any last orders?"

"Remember what I said." Pizarro glanced at the Incan nobles who would be travelling with them. "Treat your guides with whatever respect you can muster, and certainly more than they deserve. There's no point causing trouble before we've got hold of the treasure."

"What about the soldiers?"

"Keep an eye on them. Atahualpa's played straight with us so far, and if someone else is planning trouble then you'll need the protection. But don't trust them. This could be how he starts to pick us off.

"Zárate, you have your writing supplies?"

The notary nodded and opened the satchel at his side, revealing rolls of parchment and sheets of paper, three bottles of ink, and a dozen goose quills.

"Take a note of what you see along the way," Pizarro said. "And what you witness of this city of theirs. If these savages betray us, then I'll seize their capital and see how they rule without it. That means we need to know the route, and we need to know the defenses.

"Once you're there, you notarize the fact that DeSoto has taken control of the city on my behalf. If we're to bring the laws of Spain here, then I want them on my side. Keep a record of the gold you gather as well. They say this Cuzco is covered in it. I'm done waiting for Atahualpa to finish filling our treasure house — now it's down to you."

"Your will is our command," DeSoto said with a flourish of the wrist. "Myself, I'll be glad just to get off this hilltop and see the beauty of this new Eden. I am proud to be a man of action, but this place is starting to stink like an army camp."

"Don't get too excited by the wonders you see." Pizarro fought not to frown. "Keep things under control. For all our sakes."

"Of course." DeSoto turned to the other two. "Gentlemen, our carriages await."

Laughing and grinning, the three of them swaggered over to the litters. They seated themselves, their expressions turning to contentment and curiosity as they relaxed onto the cushions and examined the patterned fabric covering them. Zárate peered closely, counting something, while DeSoto leaned back, gazing around like a king from his throne. There was a moment of surprise as they were hoisted aloft on the shoulders of a dozen bronzed, muscular bearers, which turned into laughter at the absurdity of it all. The other Spaniards watched enviously as they rose in luxury above their peers.

"Until we meet again," DeSoto called out, doffing his helmet. "Gentlemen, to the city of gold!"

"God guard you on your journey," Pizarro said, raising his voice for the men all around. "Go forth in his name!" Guards forming up around them, the curious expedition headed out of the square and away.

CHAPTER TWENTY-ONE

Cuzco

Hernando DeSoto walked, naked, through the Garden of Eden. He was the first man in the world, alone beneath skies of perfect blue. As he walked the animals nuzzled up against him. The sun warmed his body.

A figure appeared from around a tree — the most shapely woman DeSoto had ever seen. She too was naked, her only adornment a dove perched on her shoulder. She smiled and swayed as she walked toward him, and DeSoto felt himself harden with desire. A rainbow arched across the sky as they approached each other. Birds sang in harmony all around. He reached out to cup her breast and-

The ground shifted beneath him and he was jolted awake, lying in the bottom of an Incan litter. He was still enflamed with passion, but there was no woman here to sate his desire. He considered dealing with it himself — after all, his companions couldn't see him lying here, with the canopy overhead shading him from the blazing sun. But the sound of grunting litter bearers was almost as off-putting as Zárate and Martín in their litters nearby, playing guessing games and inventing names for new plants. Besides, desecrating this pile of exotic cushions was more the style of Gonzalo Pizarro or the wretched Juan — DeSoto was better than that.

His erection subsiding at the thought of the Pizarros, DeSoto sat up and looked around. Every day of their journey through the mountains brought some new wonder as he sat in comfort beneath the shade of a cotton canopy, carried smoothly along by the steady hands of his porters. Lush forests dotted with brightly colored flowers. Clear streams babbling down rugged hillsides. Fields of crops completely alien to the man from dried-out Extremadura. Flocks of the distorted, long-necked sheep the locals called llamas. Martín sometimes complained of being bored, but not DeSoto. It had been an astonishing journey.

But all of that was nothing compared with the sight that greeted him now.

They were borne across a wooded ridge, between more of the lush trees that surrounded every peak. Before them, the road led down to a hillside city larger than any they had seen since leaving Spain. It seemed to shine in the sunlight spilling through the valley.

Over the next hour, he watched the city grow closer, until their path carried him into the shadow of the fortress that guarded its entrance. Three towers rose high above him, fearsome warriors staring down at him from their walls. The towers were built of stones vaster and smoother than any he had seen carved by man. It was as if the angels themselves sliced pieces from the mountainside and piled them high for God's edification. DeSoto was a noble, albeit a minor one. He had been raised around Spain's finer things. But he had never seen workmanship like this.

He could barely breath he was so excited. Standing for a better view, he ripped away the awning that protected him from the sun and swayed with the litter that shifted with the porters' footsteps. As they passed the fortress and continued into Cuzco he saw more buildings of such vast, pale stones — some elegant in their simplicity, others adorned with carvings of geometric patterns and strangely angular beasts.

By now the litters were being carried abreast, with Zárate on his left and weathered old Martín on his right. As they ascended the paved main street through the city, the most wondrous sight yet greeted them.

"Bugger me with the mainmast," Martín exclaimed. "Is that thing built of gold?"

"Gentlemen," DeSoto said, ignoring his companion's vulgarity. "Truly we are blessed to visit this world of wonders."

"You mean we're rich," Zárate said.

Ahead of them was another grand building, raised on a platform of perfectly joined stone. From the cavernous doorway facing them to the peak of its slanted roof, every inch was covered in gold.

"That's the temple we were told about, isn't it?" DeSoto asked.

Zárate nodded his head, barely looking up from the notes he was scribbling. Fresh ink stained his fingers, and a broken quill lay on the cushion beside him, a black spot seeping from it into the white cloth.

The guards fanned out around them as they entered the plaza and came to a halt before the temple. Not waiting for the porters to lower them, DeSoto leapt to the ground and kissed the flagstones.

"Praise be to God," he said, turning to Zárate. "Hurry up and make your official record — I want to get started."

The pack llamas were behind them. As DeSoto hurried to find his bags, the Incan nobles who had led them here talked with others at the head of the square. Their serious expressions grew wide-eyed as the hurried conversation unfolded, while DeSoto, half watching for signs of trouble, pulled a pair of crowbars from his bag and handed one to Martín.

A crowd had gathered, staring at the Spaniards from the edges of the square and the mouths of the streets looking onto it. Most of the men and women wore the same simple tunics and headbands the travelers had seen so often along the way. A few wore jewelry, and DeSoto made a mental note to keep an eye out for them later, once their greatest prizes had been collected.

At first glance the crowd made him nervous. There were so many of them, their expressions ranging from curiosity through fear to outright hostility. He gripped the hilt of his sword and confidence returned. They had been outnumbered in Cajamarca, but Spanish steel and Spanish spirit had put the savages to flight. They could do that again here if need be. As his confidence grew he realized that the crowds weren't a threat, they were an opportunity — an audience in front of whom he could make his mark on history.

"There's gold on another building down there." Martín pointed to one of the streets they had passed. "Think it's another of their filthy temples?"

"Doesn't matter." DeSoto grinned. "Whatever the source, these people will hand over the gold or their so-called Emperor will face the flames of hell."

"Better to start with their idolatrous temples." Zárate had appeared beside them, holding out a document quill. "I need you both to sign here."

"Can't write," Martín said. "And what the hell is idolatrous?"

"Doesn't matter," Zárate said. "It's not like they hired you for the brain work. Just make your mark, same as when you signed up for the expedition."

Leaning the sheet against the back of one of their bearers, they hastily scrawled their signatures — one a ragged cross, the other an elaborate mass of flowing lines. Then the notary thrust the record away in his satchel and pulled another crowbar from the bag.

Together, they crossed the square, the eyes of Cuzco's population upon them. In high spirits, DeSoto tipped his helmet to the gathered nobles who continued whispering frantically to each other, those who had arrived with them making some plea to the rest. Their heads bobbed up and down, feathered headdresses making them look like a flock of nervous chickens, their strange language no more than clucks and cackles to DeSoto. He wanted to laugh but didn't want to disrupt the drama of the moment.

The three Spaniards approached the steps leading up the raised platform on which the temple sat. Near the bottom of the steps, DeSoto noticed a round stain marring the pale stonework. Even in Eden, small imperfections grew.

At the top of the stairs he stopped, placed a single foot on a low wall facing the crowd, and spread his arms wide.

"People of Cuzco," he called out, and their chattering fell silent. "I know that you cannot understand a single word I say, and that I could call you all boiled lepers and filthy Englishmen for all the difference it makes to you. Nonetheless, it is my great pleasure to claim your city in the name of almighty God, his son Jesus Christ, the Holy Ghost, and, of course, King Charles of Spain. Your gold, on the other hand, I claim for Francisco Pizarro, Diego Almagro, and the excellent men who serve them."

Striding over to the temple, he placed his crowbar in the seam between two of the gold sheets on its walls. Pictures of men, animals, and plants had been hammered into the gold, and an image of the sun shone down upon them. The intricate decoration stretched high up the side of the temple, fabulous depictions of people and places, mortals and monsters, shining out from the metal. Different alloys had been used to produce different shades, so that some parts glowed a warm amber color while others were rust red, with highlights pale as silver. Zárate and Martín already had their crowbars firmly in the gaps, and as DeSoto looked at them the reflection of the scene made their eyes look gold.

"Gentlemen," he said, "let's get rich."

Together they heaved, and the first sheet of gold fell gleaming to the ground.

The crowd gasped in shock and alarm, but no one moved to stop them.

CHAPTER TWENTY-TWO

The Captives' Quarters, Cajamarca

There was fire everywhere Atahualpa looked. It fell from the heavens, scorching the earth and burning away the jungle, turning cities into charred and blackened rubble, nothing but the walls of their temples standing amid the destruction. Its roar filled his ears, drowning out the screams of the dying as Inti's wrath fell upon the Incan people.

Something else stirred, a tide of vermin sweeping out of the ocean to the west and the mountains in the north. Their teeth and claws flashed like silver — cold, pale, and deadly. The earth shook beneath the footsteps of a million claws, a tremor so deep that Atahualpa could feel it through his feet, and the chitter of their voices scratched at his ears. The stench of their bodies mixed with the smoke, choking him. The towns untouched by fire vanished beneath waves of fur and filth.

Caught between the fire on one side and the filthy creatures on the other, Atahualpa felt his skin crawl and his whole body break out in a sweat. The hairs on his head singed and curled. He could smell his flesh roasting in the heat and hear the scratching of claws coming ever closer. As he turned from one threat to the other, unable to choose, the vermin fell upon him. They ripped out his eyes, even as the flames ignited his feet.

The Emperor jolted awake, crying out in alarm.

Moonlight fell through the window of the room in which he slept, illuminating a rat sitting on the floor, its tail twitching as it stared at him. Suddenly, something startled the creature, and it darted away into the darkness.

"Atahualpa." Cuyoc laid a gentle hand on his shoulder. He had not heard her move from her bed on the other side of the room, but he was not surprised to find her at his side. Such silent movement, appearing as if by magic, this was her way. "Are you unwell?"

He shook his head and pulled the blankets up around him. After the heat of the inferno, the cool night air made him shiver.

"It was a dream," he said. "An omen of what is upon us."

"Tell me," she said.

Atahualpa leaned back against the wall while his sister positioned herself cross-legged on the floor in front of him. Like the rest of the room, she was cast into darkness, a shadow rather than a human being. After weeks of captivity, he had felt increasingly reticent to speak to anyone about anything. Asked to tell his sister about his dream, he felt both absurd and ashamed.

"It was nothing," he said at last, though he knew it was not true.

"Tell me," she said again, her voice soft and insistent.

Reluctantly, he began to tell her about the fire and the fangs that had haunted his night. The more he talked the faster the words came, until the whole nightmare came tumbling out, and with it the harsh conclusion to which he had awoken.

"I have to make a choice," he said. "I cannot serve both the Spanish and the gods."

"You are not serving the Spanish," Cuyoc said. "You are surviving them."

Atahualpa snorted.

"Tell them that," he said. "Have you seen the way they treat me? At the beginning, there was some respect — fear even. They knew that I could bring a great army upon them, if I only had the nerve to risk my death at their hands. But their weapons and their horses turned me into a coward, shrinking from the shock of what I had seen. Now they treat me like that coward, not the mighty warrior who brought Huascar's army to its knees. They are open in making demands. One more week and they will be ordering me around like a servant."

"I wonder if it's just the gold," Cuyoc said. "The more that arrives, the more confident they become. It is as if they were drawing out the divine power of the metal, corrupting it to fuel their pride."

"Is that how they have beaten us?" Atahualpa asked in alarm. "Some dark sorcery?"

"No," she said. "Hernando has taught me much about their ways, and there is no magic at work here — just the confidence that comes with power. You remember that feeling, don't you?"

Atahualpa cast his mind back to the conquests he had undertaken in the north. The clash of weapons and the thud of bodies. The screams of his enemies as they fell before him. Blood, sweat, and the smoke of burning villages. Watching men plead for their lives and knowing that the power to decide was all his. The joy of victory and the way that each triumph built upon the last. More recently even, the way his heart had soared at finally bringing Huascar to his knees, despite the bitterness and loss that war had brought. There was no feeling like it in the world.

"I remember," he said. "But it is harder to make the memory into something of substance. I used to believe that the whole world was mine. Now I feel...expendable."

"That is how you are to the Spanish, not to us," Cuyoc said.

"It does not matter," Atahualpa said, as he finally accepted a thought he had long been denying. "Once they have gold up to that line they will dispose of me or make more demands until I have nothing left to give."

"It doesn't have to be that way," Cuyoc said. "You can lead us through this darkness and back into Inti's light."

"Against their guns?" He sank his face into his hands. "Against their swords and their horses?"

"Against their cruelty. Against their indignities. Against the way they treat us all like their playthings — you, me, your people, our gods. Where is the respect an emperor is due? Think of how they treat you, with their lies and their insults."

Fire began to flicker again in Atahualpa's heart. A flame of anger that grew with every second, as if his sister had blown upon the dying embers of his soul, bringing back some of the heat and vigor he once had. Still wrapped in blankets, he stood and crossed the room to where a pile of coarse strings lay, ready to be knotted into quipu as coded messages. Sitting down beside them, he picked up a string and ran it through his fingers, feeling the rough threads. His body was calm, but his mind raged. He would not be caught between the fire and the vermin. He would be the flame that burned away their filth.

"Can I help?" Cuyoc was there again, a figure of wisdom appearing silently at his side.

"One for each of my generals," Atahualpa said quietly. "A servant will carry them out in the morning. Each one must say that I suspect treachery, and to prepare the armies to rescue me."

"You should be careful," Cuyoc said, sitting down and beginning to tie the knots. "Only send to those of whose loyalty you are absolutely certain. Many might use your weakness against you or turn the foreigners to their gain."

"Whereas you would just turn one of them to your bed." He regretted the words the moment they were out of his mouth. But an emperor did not take back what he said, least of all when it was true.

Cuyoc's fingers fell still, a quipu half knotted in her hands.

"Whatever else I feel," she said, "I am loyal to you."

"I know," Atahualpa said, the fire burning within him. He could not yet take up arms and return to being a warrior, as he longed to, but he could at least take action.

Together they sat silently in the dark, tying messages and waiting for the dawn.

Atahualpa would make the Spaniards burn.

CHAPTER TWENTY-THREE

Cajamarca Town Square

Pizarro watched the caracara circling above the town square. He'd grown attached to the birds, in as far as he ever grew attached to anything that wasn't a sign of God or his own growing fortune. There was something clear-cut about the creatures, with their white and black feathers and their predictable behavior, swooping overhead looking for flesh that they could scavenge. He imagined himself as one of those birds, soaring above this pitiful excuse for a civilization, waiting for his moment to sweep down and take what he wanted.

On a whim, he'd taken to throwing scraps of meat onto his rooftop after meals, giving the caracara something to feast on. They had signaled his shift in fortune — there was no sense in antagonizing them.

While Pizarro indulged in this one small piece of superstition, Juan reveled in signs and omens.

"Curse those creatures," he said peering up at the birds. "The almanacs always say that carrion are unlucky."

He spat over his left shoulder and crossed himself.

"How many of your almanac writers have been to the New World?" Pizarro asked.

"None, probably," Juan said. "Aside from our Zárate, scribes aren't an adventurous sort."

"Then who's to say that the omens aren't different out here?" Pizarro said. "Or that they aren't all nonsense for superstitious old women."

"Who are you calling a woman?" Juan's hand went to his sword.

"Who do you think you are threatening?" Pizarro reached for his. He knew this wouldn't come to blows, but it still felt good to let his blood rise after all these weeks of waiting and counting their gold.

Juan slumped and stomped away. There weren't many men he had to let insult him, and he had never learnt to leave such a situation with good grace.

It was a strange juxtaposition, the surly Spaniard against a backdrop of soaring mountains and lush jungle. But Pizarro's world was full of strange juxtapositions, like the two figures approaching him across the square.

In theory, it was good that Hernando was getting to know Atahualpa. The closer the youngest Pizarro got to the Incan Emperor, the more information they might get about these people, their nation, and their wealth. But Hernando's ease around the Emperor and his sister made Pizarro uneasy. It was blurring the clear line between his people, the Spaniards, and the Incan community, this nation of savages he was bringing to heel.

"Governor Pizarro," Atahualpa said slowly as he approached. The Emperor had picked up very little Spanish, and his accent was terrible. It was hardly surprising that he stumbled over these longer words. But he was trying to fit in with real Christian civilization, and even if his attempts were embarrassing, they were at least a step toward saving these people for God and Spain.

"Emperor Atahualpa." Pizarro nodded his head in greeting. "Hernando."

His brother smiled and nodded back. Around them, the men tasked with guarding Atahualpa formed a loose, watchful circle. The Incas had still made no attempt at a rescue, but that was no reason for the conquistadors to let down their guard.

The Emperor said something in his own language. He was looking at Pizarro but gesturing at Hernando, speaking slowly so that the conquistador could translate. The whole time he spoke he treated them to a warm smile, but Pizarro caught a fragment of something colder in his eyes.

"You understand all this?" Pizarro said as the Emperor finished.

"Enough to get the general message," Hernando said. "Atahualpa asks if you will play chess with him. I have been teaching him the game, and he has taken to it with great skill."

"Does he really ask, or does he demand?" Pizarro had seen enough of Atahualpa to notice the similarities between them. The Emperor might be doing his best to befriend his captors, but he still didn't strike Pizarro as a man who asked so much as he ordered.

"I didn't catch the nuance," Hernando said diplomatically. "But he would very much like a game with you — he's been saying so all morning."

Taking a long step forward, Pizarro looked Atahualpa in the eye, the two of them less than a foot apart. They stared at each other — captive and conqueror, emperor and adventurer, both warriors and leaders of men. Neither flinched nor looked away.

"What do you want?" Pizarro said, his voice little more than a whisper. "What are you playing at, with your smiles and your games of chess?"

Atahualpa just looked back at him, smiling that same smile, an expression that could have convinced anyone but the most cynical of human beings.

Pizarro didn't trust it.

"Tell him no," he said at last. "I have no time for games."

"It could be useful," Hernando said. "They say that soft words can soothe the most nervous of beasts."

"They also say that virgins can tame unicorns," Pizarro said. "But there aren't any virgins left in this land."

"I fear you've been spending too long around Juan," Hernando said with a nervous grin. "You're starting to sound like him."

"And I fear you're spending too much time with our captive," Pizarro replied. "Remember, we aren't friends, he isn't on our side, and we didn't come all this way to read poetry and pick flowers. Play chess with him if you must, and learn what you can from it, but keep your sword sharp and your wits about you."

"Always!" Hernando said. "Now if you won't play, then we will."

He said something to Atahualpa, who frowned, then smiled again. He gave Pizarro another brief nod and then followed Hernando away, the guards circling around them as they spoke in halting Incan.

Looking up at the skies, Pizarro saw the caracara still circling and eyeing the town below.

"I know you, brother." Gonzalo stepped out of the shadows of a doorway. For a mass of muscles and scars, he could be surprisingly stealthy. "You aren't stupid enough to trust that gold-grabbing bastard."

"Is everyone in this town set on disturbing my peace?" Pizarro asked. He was resigned to people needing his attention — that was the price of power — but after the previous conversation he wanted quiet in which to think.

"Sorry," Gonzalo said, backing away. "I didn't mean to interrupt, just to see if I could help."

"You want to help?" Pizarro considered rejecting the offer. Gonzalo's cunning was limited and often poorly aimed. But then, he would work hard if he thought he could gain by it. "Talk with the other men. Find out what else our captive has been doing. He's up to something, and I want to know what."

CHAPTER TWENTY-FOUR

Cajamarca

There were more Spaniards than usual outside the house in which Atahualpa was kept captive. Alarmed at the sight, Cuyoc approached cautiously. She wondered, "Had something terrible happened? Or was it about to?"

The Spaniards seemed less alert than usual, for all their numbers. They were grinning and talking among themselves, winking and nudging each other in their armored ribs. Juan Pizarro, perhaps the most odious man she had ever met, leaned against a building at the far side of the street; his gaze fixed on the doorway of the home that had become a prison.

The curtain in the doorway was pulled aside, and Cuyoc realized what she should have known from the start. Only one thing drew men in such a way, and that thing was a woman.

Despite herself, Cuyoc felt a pang of jealousy as she watched Quispe emerge from the house. It was not that she wanted Spaniards leering after her as they were leering after her sister. But there was a power in drawing men's gazes as Quispe did, and a pride that could be taken in it. When she was younger, Cuyoc had that level of allure. Now she mustered her power by other means, and the pride was all but forgotten.

Quispe smiled as she looked up and saw Cuyoc. It was a light, pretty smile that suited her delicate features. Not exactly innocent, but with freshness and a young woman's appeal. They greeted each other briefly and then Quispe continued on down the hill, accompanied by a pair of Incan guards and a close following of Spaniards. Cuyoc continued into the darkness of the house, shaking her head as she went.

Atahualpa sprawled lethargically on a pile of cushions at the back of the room.

"So it was that sort of visit," Cuyoc said, seating herself on a pile of blankets and rugs.

"What?" Atahualpa frowned and then laughed. "No, I decided long ago not to marry Quispe, just as I did you. I know it would benefit the purity of the royal bloodline, but she is far more useful as a political tool. I want to keep her untouched, to bind a powerful man to me by marriage."

"Then you should keep her away from the Spaniards," Cuyoc said. "Their intentions are powerful, but far from pure."

A deep sigh escaped Atahualpa as he sat up. His expression was haggard, his once bright eyes dim. It broke Cuyoc's heart to see the strength of their family and their empire broken this way. That he was her beloved brother only made it worse.

"The endless politics exhausts me." He pressed his hands to his face. "The pretense of pleasure, the careful maneuvering, the smiles, and the strain of observing and calculating every last detail. I long to have an axe in my hand and a foe who I can fight instead of having to befriend. This is Huascar's sort of work, not mine."

"You'll learn," Cuyoc said. "I did."

"I hope not," Atahualpa said, fearing that if she were right his soul would shrivel away to something worse than Huascar had been. He looked out through the doorway and forced a smile onto his face. "Speaking of learning, here comes our Spanish tutor."

Hernando entered the room, his chessboard held out before him. He bowed to the Emperor, and then to Cuyoc.

Was it her imagination, or did he bow more deeply to her, and with a more generous smile? Didn't his eyes linger on her in a way they shouldn't have?

A long forgotten pride stirred in her heart, and she smiled back.

∼

Gonzalo let out a groan of pleasure. Spent, he rolled off the Incan serving woman. The cushions that made up his improvised bed were incredibly comfortable, one of the many treasures he'd taken from the locals, along with the girl herself. As he stretched out, she pulled a blanket over herself and curled up against the wall, her shoulders shaking in a silent sob.

A silhouette shifted in the doorway. Gonzalo sat up and reached for his sword.

"My turn now," Juan said, walking into the small stone room they shared. He licked his lips as he looked down at the woman.

"Were you watching me, you pervert?" Gonzalo said.

"You're calling me a pervert?" Juan said. "I know your tastes, and they're just as twisted as mine."

He started fumbling with his belt, then stopped as the woman turned her face to look up at him.

"Not this plain piece of flesh again," he said.

"Not much fresh meat up this mountain," Gonzalo said. "What do you want, Princess Cuyoc?"

"Oh no, it's the other sister I want." Juan picked up a large clay bottle from the corner of the room and pulled out the stopper. He drank the bottle dry, foam dribbling down his chin, then lowered it with a frown. "I'm sick of this local shit. When are we getting some real wine like we had back home?"

"When you swim back to Spain for it." Gonzalo wiped himself on a rag and pulled on his hose.

"Do you think the Emperor keeps her for himself?" Juan asked, finishing the sentence with a long belch.

"Keeps who?" Gonzalo asked.

"Quispe," Juan said. "The stunning one."

"She looks too innocent for that." Gonzalo picked up another of the bottles. "Besides, she's his sister."

"Doesn't matter to these heathen bastards," Juan said. "Hernando told me that the Emperor's meant to marry his sisters, to keep the royal bloodline strong. Except most of his brothers and sisters are half-brothers and half-sisters, so the full sisters are extra special for purity. Not that she can really be all that pure — the innocent looking girls are always the filthiest. I plan to give that one a good cleaning." He grabbed his crotch for emphasis. "A good cleaning, see?"

"I got it." Gonzalo rolled his eyes. Even by Juan's standard, that line was getting old. "But you won't get her. Francisco will save that bit for himself, you wait and see."

"What will I save for myself?" Francisco Pizarro stood in the doorway, arms folded across his chest.

The happiness that had filled Gonzalo drained away. That stance and that tone of voice meant only one thing — they were in trouble again.

"Precious little Princess Quispe," Juan said, either oblivious or ignoring their older brother's mood. "Or aren't hot little things your type anymore?"

"No one is to touch Quispe," Francisco said. "Or any other member of Atahualpa's family. And you two need to rein your antics in."

"What?" Juan said in outrage. "What's the point in coming here if it's not to take what we want?"

"Think with your head for once." Francisco strode up to Juan and stared him straight in the eye. Juan glared back for a moment, then looked away. "There's more at stake here than wine and women. We're playing for a whole empire, our fortunes and our futures. So cut back on the thefts, and the women, and the beatings I know you two have lain on the locals. You'll get your chance, just not yet."

He turned and strode away.

"Arsehole," Juan muttered once Francisco was out of earshot.

"Don't worry," Gonzalo said, laying a hand on his shoulder. "We'll get what we're after soon enough. And while you wait, there's a plain little someone waiting for you in my bed."

Juan looked up with a grin.

"You're always good to me, Gonzalo."

Beneath her pile of blankets, the Incan girl closed her eyes.

CHAPTER TWENTY-FIVE

The Edge of Cajamarca

There were few things Hernando enjoyed more than sitting in the sunshine, waiting for Cuyoc. From the moment he sat down, he never knew when she would appear, suddenly and silently, by his side. Each moment filled with anticipation, right up to the revelation of her presence.

"You saw me?" she said as she appeared on the wall beside him, with its view down the hill.

"I wish," he said. "Had I seen you coming I could have enjoyed your presence for longer. It would be like watching the sky lighten before the dawn."

She looked at him in confusion, so he pointed at her, then the clear blue sky above, and mimed the sun's rays spreading out around them. Cuyoc blushed and looked away.

It amazed him how much Spanish she had picked up already and how much of her language he understood. Neither knew enough of the other's language for a full conversation, but they got by. Between them they spoke a private mixture of Spanish, Incan, and mime — conversations where meaning became tangled but carried more emotional weight than any others in his life. Conversations that no one around them could entirely follow.

They sat together for a while, watching the scenery and teaching each other new words. A pair of caracara circled in the sky overhead, their flight a thing of strange beauty as they drew closer to one another. Even nature was filled with love.

Incan messengers passed them by, running up and down the hill. He found the dedication of Atahualpa's servants inspiring, the way they stood by him in this moment of crisis. Even their clothes had an elegant simplicity — the blocky patterns of red, blue, and white drawing in the eye. As they passed he asked questions, and he and Cuyoc ended up teaching each other words for colors, leaning closer as they talked, until her face was only inches from his and all he could think about was the scent of her and the smoothness of her skin.

She nudged him and pointed, frowning as she looked toward the road out of town. Juan stood, Gonzalo and a few others around him, blocking that road. Another group was coming up from the valley below — Quispe and a handful of attendants.

A sense of dread took hold of Hernando.

"Go get your brother," he said, hoping she understood enough of his words to know how to act. "And send for Francisco. Quickly."

Without a sound, she vanished. Checking the sword at his side, he leapt to his feet and strode toward Juan.

As he hurried, a stone rolled out from beneath his foot. His ankle twisted beneath him and he stumbled. Regaining his balance, he hobbled forwards, too late to stop what was coming, but close enough to see it begin.

Seeing their path blocked, the Incas stopped only yards

from the Spaniards.

"Hello, princess." Juan stepped forward. Reaching out, he placed a hand against the side of her face. Her sweet smile, second only to Cuyoc's among the women Hernando had met, turned into a look of terror. "I think it's time we got to know one another."

A tear ran from the corner of her eye, glittering as it caught the sunlight. Juan caught it on his finger, then licked that finger with a grin before reaching out to lay his hand on her throat.

"I'm going to make you scream, you stuck up little bitch," Juan said.

Quispe shook her head, her eyes fixed on Juan, pleading with him in words he couldn't understand. But he understood the tone well enough for his grin to widen.

"Juan!" Hernando called out, sick to his stomach but still too slow.

One of the Incan guards slapped Juan's arm aside, then stepped between Quispe and the Spaniards, his teeth bared in fury. Two of the other Incas raised bronze-headed clubs. The rest, unarmed servants, raised their fists or picked up rocks from the road. Every one of their faces filled with outrage.

Juan looked down at his hand and then back up at the Inca. Around him, there was the soft, menacing sound of steel across cloth as swords were drawn.

"You don't touch me, you heathen bastard," Juan said, his face a picture of fury. "No one touches me."

His sword glittered in the sunlight as he raised it. The Incan guard stood firm, holding up a stone-lined club that was the closest the locals had to a sword. Quispe backed away, her eyes wide with fear.

"Juan, stop this madness." Hernando limped up to his brother and grabbed him by the shoulder.

There was a blur of movement. Juan's off hand collided with the underside of Hernando's chin, knocking him down in the dirt, his mouth full of blood. Even as he flung off his brother, Juan was lunging forward, blood lust lighting up his face as he slashed and darted at the guard with his blade.

In an instant, everybody was moving. Servants ran screaming. Guards and Spaniards clashed. Steel and bronze collided. Rocks hurtled through the air.

Quispe screamed as she hid behind her servants, but one of the Spaniards darted around and grabbed her arm, flinging her from her feet. There was a sickening thud as she hit the ground and lay cowering before a man twice her size.

Hernando's head spun as he forced himself to his feet. Most of the brawl was like so many others he had been part of — men seeking to wound and intimidate rather than kill. In the streets of Spain that was a way to avoid the noose, as well as the time in hell that came from the mortal sin of murder. Here and now it was habit, men blowing off steam rather than killing for conquest.

But right in front of him was the exception, Juan and the guard going at it with fury fuelling their every move.

The Inca was good. For every attack Juan launched he was ready with a parry. He spotted bluffs and feints and didn't let himself get drawn in. He found space to attack, forcing Juan to relent in his own offensive.

But it wasn't enough. Juan was fighting downhill. He had

great strength and at least as much skill as his opponent. The devilish glee on his face spoke to an energy unparalleled even among the conquistadors. Most of all, he had a steel blade — lighter, faster, and more deadly than his opponent's weapon. When the Inca caught him with a glancing blow, it clanged off his breastplate or bruised his arm. When he got such a hit against the Inca, blood flowed, spattering the ground as flaps of skin and flesh hung loose. The ground grew red and slippery, and the guard slid to one knee. Juan laughed and raised his blade for a final strike.

Leaping forwards, Hernando grabbed his brother's arm. The two of them grappled for a long moment, but Juan in his full fury was a force Hernando had never been able to match. Hernando was forced back, his ankle gave way beneath him again, and he fell with a grunt.

"You lousy piece of treacherous shit." Juan raised his sword again. The sun caught his face from the side, sinking his eye sockets into shadow, giving him the appearance of a leering skull — death itself coming for Hernando. Yet his heart was focused on the terrible screams still coming from Quispe as she struggled with the Spaniard tearing away her clothes.

Hoof beats came thundering toward them.

"Stop this at once!" Francisco Pizarro's voice rang in Hernando's ears.

For a moment he thought that Juan would still strike, such was the fury in his face. But slowly, reluctantly, his brother lowered his blade.

Everyone turned to look at Pizarro.

"What is the meaning of this?" he said.

No one replied.

"You!" Pizarro pointed at Juan. "Is it true? Did you try to seize that woman?"

The brothers glared at each other, both trembling and red-faced with rage. The only sounds were Quispe's whimpers and the dripping of blood from Juan's sword.

"Answer me!" Pizarro said.

"Yes," Juan said through gritted teeth.

"What about them?" Pizarro said, pointing at the Incas but looking at Hernando. "Did they strike first or did they wait for him?"

Hernando hesitated, thinking back to the start of the fight. The guard knocking aside Juan's hand. In his heart, he knew that this was all Juan's doing, but he would not lie to Francisco.

"It depends on what you consider a strike," he said.

"It depends on nothing!" Pizarro stared around at the Spaniards, most of whom looked ashamed or afraid in the face of their commander. "This does not happen again, you understand me? There is more at stake here than some brown-faced girl, and I will kill any man who jeopardizes that for me.

"And you." He looked again at Hernando. "You tell your heathen friends, any that step out of line will be slain. If they're lucky, death will be the worst of it."

He wheeled his horse around and rode back into town where Cuyoc and Atahualpa stood waiting for him, the Emperor barely concealing his shock. Seeing the look Cuyoc gave him, Hernando felt like a hero out of myth, an Odysseus or Heracles protecting innocents from the monsters of the deep. He smiled at her, his Helen of Troy, and pushed himself up out of the dirt.

Juan kicked his arm out from under him. His chin hit the ground and he tasted blood.

"One of these days I'll be the one guarding your back in battle," Juan said, his eyes burning with fury. "What do you think will happen then?"

As he stomped off, he spat at Quispe, her whole body shaking. Cuyoc helped her up from the blood stained dirt.

CHAPTER TWENTY-SIX

The Ransom Room, Cajamarca

There was so much gold in the Ransom Room that there was no space to stand. Cups and bowls, necklaces and earrings, misshapen scraps found in workshops and elaborately hammered sheets torn off of temple walls — all of it was piled up together in a vast, gleaming heap.

Atahualpa's stomach tightened as he struggled to process his warring emotions. The sight was so warped it unsettled him to his core, holy metal piled up in a desecrated heap to buy off these foreign intruders. The divine and the mundane turned upon their heads, conduits of cosmic power used for spoils of war.

Mixed in with his shame was a deep sense of relief. The gold had reached the line set at the start of his imprisonment. He had fulfilled his side of the agreement. If these men could be trusted then soon he would be free to go. Free of these barbarians and their dark ways. He would return to court, to his place of safety and power, and remove them from his realm. He would take his family and his supporters away from the danger these men presented. He would cast off the shroud of low politics, take up the axe and bring war upon his foes.

Trusting the Spaniards to keep their word was a hard thing, but if any of them had honor then it was Pizarro, the man in charge. Without that trust, however desperate it was, Atahualpa would be left without hope.

Stepping aside, the Emperor let one of the Spaniards through the doorway. The man flung a panel of beaten gold up on top of the heap, the holes where it had been fixed to a temple wall visible at its corners. There was a clang, and the man walked back out. He didn't lower his gaze in Atahualpa's presence. He ignored him.

The sun was low in the sky, and its light shone orange and red across the heaped treasure, turning it from cold metal into raging flames. The same flames that roiled in Atahualpa's heart. But this was not the time to give way to anger or pain. Now was the time for control and to put matters to rest.

Turning from the Ransom Room, Atahualpa saw Francisco Pizarro standing on the far side of the square, an interpreter by his side. The Spaniard had kept as careful a count of the growing pile of gold as Atahualpa had. It was no surprise to find him here, ready for the conversation that must follow. For all that Atahualpa loathed in the invaders, he had to acknowledge strength of will in their leader, a willingness to face whatever came. Pizarro was not a man to avoid awkwardness or confrontation.

They walked toward each other, the gaunt grey ghost of a man from beyond the ocean and the fiery Emperor of the Incas. In the middle of the square they stopped. Atahualpa looked into the eyes of the man of iron.

"Tell him that the Ransom Room is full to the line, as I promised," the Emperor said. "Now, as we agreed, he is to let me go."

The translator spoke in the language of the foreigners, something Atahualpa was just beginning to grasp. Cuyoc could have conveyed his words better, if she had Hernando to help her. But she was already too entangled with these people, and Atahualpa did not want her further involved. These events had left him with so little of his pride, he had to prove to himself that he could do this without her.

Pizarro did not speak in response to the words. He stepped slowly past Atahualpa, beckoning the Emperor to follow. So this was how it would be, Atahualpa thought. Pizarro was drawing out the moment after all, unwilling to let go.

At the doorway of the Ransom Room they stopped. Pizarro stared at the gold, one finger tapping on the hilt of his sword. Then he pointed at the ceiling, another four feet above the original line.

Even before the translator spoke, Atahualpa knew that he was betrayed. The Spaniard looked at him with cold, demanding patience, while Atahualpa's cheeks burned with shame.

In this room were the most sacred items of his entire empire. Panels from temples and statues of gods, cups from divine ceremonies and jewelry glorifying the heavens. Here were the pieces that Inca nobles had worn every day of their lives as a sign of worship. He had asked them to give up possessions worth more than mere wealth could ever represent, and they had done it. It had humiliated him to ask, and yet delighted him to see how willingly they would sacrifice for their emperor. The thought of handing it over had sickened him, but at least it had been toward a purpose.

Now that purpose was gone. All this gold, the prized possessions of nobles and the sacred ornaments of temples, it was not enough. Fill the rest of the room, the Spaniard was saying, and you can go free. Just a few more feet of gold. You have shamed yourself and your nation this far, what's a little more?

He listened to the garbled, nervous version of the young translator, not out of interest but for form's sake. Then he forced himself to nod his head and speak in agreement. A stiff smile spread across Pizarro's face. Then the conquistador strode away across the square, night falling around him.

Atahualpa stood staring after his rapacious foe.

"I warned you that they could not be trusted." Cuyoc's voice came from the shadows. "They are like spiders creeping across the web — dark, grasping, hungry."

She emerged into the twilight outside the Ransom Room and laid a hand on her brother's arm.

"I am sorry, Atahualpa," she said.

"They never intended to let me go," he said, staring after the vanished Spaniard. "They never will. How ironic that you, who have grown closest to these savages, warned me against trusting their words."

"It does not fill me with joy to be right," Cuyoc said. "But I am relieved to see my brother receive enlightenment, however bitter it may be. Perhaps now is the time to muster your forces, to take control of events."

Insects stirred outside of town, their chirping drifting into the square. To Atahualpa, everyone seemed to say, "I told you so."

"Gather the quipu strings," he said quietly. "I must send

messages to my generals."

"And what will these messages say?" Cuyoc said.

Atahualpa said, "Attack."

CHAPTER TWENTY-SEVEN

Cajamarca

Cuyoc's footsteps echoed around the empty servants' hut. The servants were all eating their evening meal, or serving Atahualpa and visiting nobles. She wondered if her brother had told the others about Pizarro's new demand. Some would be angry, she was sure, others resigned. Few could be surprised. They had all seen the disdain with which the Spaniards treated them.

Sometimes even each other, given the way Juan and Gonzalo watched Hernando.

Thinking of him gave her pause. What would happen to him when Atahualpa called his armies down upon the invaders? The thought of Hernando dying upset her, though she would happily have seen all his companions slain. She should find a way to protect him. He could prove useful if more foreigners came. After all, he knew their language and was more reasonable than most. There were good reasons to keep him alive.

There were unused quipu strings in a basket in the corner of the room. Few of the servants had the skills or cause to record anything, but one of those here was an educated man tasked with managing supplies. He needed the strings for his record keeping and calculations.

She hesitated as she took the strings from the basket. Would the Spaniards notice their absence? They must look in here sometimes, if only to make sure there were no weapons hidden around the room. What was the likelihood that they would become suspicious at the missing string? Should she find a way to hide what she had taken?

This was beyond mere calculation. It was paranoia. She doubted most of the Spaniards had even worked out what the quipu were. They were certainly not keeping track of them.

Carrying a fistful of string, she turned toward the door. A slender figure stood there, his sudden appearance making her heart jump. But she kept her alarm hidden. It was easy enough when she realized who the new arrival was.

"Manco." She smiled in greeting. Though they did not share a mother, she was fond of her younger brother. He had always been more pleasant than his full brother Huascar. The light of a scheming mind sometimes burned in his eyes, but never as brightly as it had in Huascar's, or in the eyes of many in the court. "The servants are away serving food."

"Then why are you here?" he asked. There was innocence in the question, his expression that of a youth barely at the start of manhood.

"I have messages to send." Even in acts of deception, it was best to make use of the truth. "I came to collect quipu."

"Can I help?" he asked. "I may not be fast, but I can still tie messages."

"There is no need," Cuyoc said. The fewer people that knew what was happening, the better. And though she liked

Manco, she knew Atahualpa did not. It was only her word that had saved Manco from sharing Huascar's fate when the civil war ended. "Go and eat. I will be with you soon."

"Of course," he said, eyes narrowing. "Why would the mighty Atahualpa ever want my help?"

∼

Pizarro stood on the roof of one of the houses, looking up at the night sky. The same stars that had allowed the three wise men to navigate their way to Bethlehem had allowed him and his followers to navigate their way here. Halfway around the world to see a priceless treasure in a humble hut. Truly, history had come back around. Except that this time the visitors were receiving gold, not giving it away. Unlike those wise men, Pizarro didn't have to make himself poorer to glorify God. They may have been wise, but he was more cunning.

There was a musty smell up here, despite the breeze blowing off the mountains. The caracara had left their droppings, in exchange for the meat he had cast upwards for them. It was a reminder that, no matter where you went, filth was never far. Stars were everywhere, and so was shit.

He thought back to the encounter with Atahualpa earlier. Had the Emperor accepted the demand for more gold too easily? Pizarro had expected some sort of resistance, futile as it would have been. Perhaps their captive really had given up the will to fight. After all, he could hardly hope to survive any violence that broke out. There might be countless hordes of barbarians in the valley below, ready to answer their master's call, but it only took one blade to slay a prisoner, even when that prisoner was an emperor.

"Francisco!" Gonzalo called out from the doorway below.

"You had better not be interrupting me because you're out of wine," Pizarro replied.

"May devils piss on your eyes," Gonzalo said. "Do you want your message or not?"

"What message?" Pizarro asked. Not waiting for a reply, he crossed the roof and reached for the ladder down the side of the building.

"One of the locals wants to see you," Gonzalo said. "Barely more than a kid, but I've seen him wearing gold, so he's someone who matters."

The ladder creaked beneath Pizarro as he climbed down. He would have someone strengthen it in the morning. Some of the men should tend to the cannons too — he didn't think they'd been cleaned and checked since the battle. Overseeing that should have been someone else's job, but trusting the thugs he'd brought with him to do their job was a sure way to get killed.

Reaching the bottom, he turned to see Gonzalo, a clay jug in his hand. There was wine in his beard and disgruntlement on his face, lit as it was by the brands that burned around the perimeter of the Spanish barracks hall. Behind him stood a young aristocrat who Pizarro had seen coming in and out of town, dressed in a red and white tunic and with feathers in his headdress. One of the translators stood behind them both, shifting from foot to foot, his eyes downcast.

"This is him." Gonzalo jerked a thumb at the Inca. "Now can I get back to my dinner?"

Pizarro grabbed the jug from his brother's hand and took a drink. The local wine had a strange taste, but it was better than drinking river water.

"Next time you show some respect, or I'll break this over your head." He waved the jug at Gonzalo. "Now get back to whatever you were shoveling down your throat."

As Gonzalo stomped away, the Inca stepped forwards. He couldn't have been more than seventeen years old, his skin baby soft, and he showed none of the lean maturity that marked Atahualpa and his favorites.

The youth said something and held out a long cord. Pizarro took the cord and ran it through his fingers, peering at the knots all along its length. From his visitor's expression, he felt sure it had more significance than crop growth recordings.

"Manco Inca, brother of Huascar and Atahualpa, greets you," the translator said. "He says that this string is a message from Atahualpa to one of his generals. He says that he killed one of Atahualpa's messengers to take it for you."

"And why does he think that I will care about this?" Pizarro looked at the soft boy again, re-evaluating him. Something more than firelight gleamed in Manco's eyes.

Words went back and forth in the local tongue. At last the translator spoke in Spanish again, his voice tight with fear.

"Atahualpa is planning an attack."

CHAPTER TWENTY-EIGHT

Francisco Pizarro's Lodgings, Cajamarca

"What's this all about?" Juan said as he staggered through the door into one of the best-maintained houses in Cajamarca.

Pizarro nailed his brother with a deadly glare.

"Leave your wine outside," he said.

"Why should I?" Juan said. "It's late and I'm thirsty."

"Leave it outside or leave your hand with it."

Juan's face crumpled. Pizarro could almost see the thoughts battling each other in his expression — slow, primitive things subservient to instinct.

At last, Juan reached a decision. Stepping outside, he set his cup down next to the doorway with a clunk, then came back into the house. Excitement stirred in his eyes.

"You sound serious," he said. "Is there going to be a fight?"

"Perhaps." Pizarro sat in a simple armchair in the corner of the room, next to a fire that burned with low menace. The locals didn't use much furniture, but one of his men had been a carpenter before he became a conquistador, and when it became clear that they would be in the town for some time he had made the chair and other furniture for Pizarro. It was more comfortable than the rickety benches they had assembled in other buildings, and in a land without decent seating, it seemed almost as stately as a throne.

Juan looked around at the lack of cushions or seats, then shrugged and went to lean against the wall by the fire. His fingers drummed against the handle of the long dagger he kept in his belt.

Friar Vicente was the next to arrive, his expression sober and serious, a Bible clutched in his hands. It was the same Bible he had carried on the first day in Cajamarca, its cover stained with blood. Hernando DeSoto, recently returned from Cuzco, accompanied him. In the low, flickering light of the fire, the sunken eyes of Almagro's lieutenant turned into black pits, like the eyes of a skull. Finally came Gonzalo and Hernando Pizarro, the former staggering, the latter holding him up long enough to get into the house. Hernando turned and closed the curtain behind them.

"What's this about?" Gonzalo asked, crossing the room to stand next to Juan.

"That's what I said," Juan replied, as if they had both stumbled upon some deep insight. "I want answers."

"Lower your voices," Pizarro hissed.

A stony silence fell across the assembled men, and their expressions turned to intensity. Warrior instincts took over, hands tightening around the handles of their weapons. The priest shifted his footing, looked at his Bible, and stood taller.

Pizarro had them well trained.

"What do you know about Atahualpa's brother Manco?" he said, looking at Hernando.

"He's young," Hernando said, stroking his beard. "One of the youngest of the family. You know they had a civil war just before we arrived?"

"Bloody savages," Juan said.

The friar crossed himself.

"Manco was on the other side," Hernando said. "I think because he was full brother to Atahualpa's opponent, Huascar. But he didn't do anything important — I'm not sure he even fought. And Atahualpa forgave him — Cuyoc told me that as proof that her brother is magnanimous in victory."

"If Cuyoc said it then it must be true," Gonzalo said in a bitter tone.

"Give me a chance and I'll get the truth out of her." Juan grinned and started thrusting with his belt buckle.

Juan and Gonzalo burst out laughing. DeSoto raised an amused eyebrow. Hernando and the friar both frowned, though only one of them clenched his hand around a sword hilt.

Pizarro was on his feet and across the room in two strides. Grabbing Juan by the throat he slammed him up against the wall, his feet dangling by the fire. Juan's eyes went wide with alarm and he made desperate, choking sounds.

"I don't care worth a piss about Hernando's little strumpet," Pizarro said. "But you don't bring your drunken prick-wagging into this business. Understand?"

Juan nodded. Eyes still fixed on his troublesome brother, Pizarro let him go.

"The civil war makes sense of it," he said, returning to his seat. "Manco came to me this evening with this."

He held up the knotted string.

"A quipu," Hernando said, stepping closer to peer at it.

"You know what it is?" Pizarro asked. He watched Hernando closely, vigilant for any sign that his brother was holding back. He was closer to the Incas than the rest of them, and there was a risk that his motives had become muddled.

"I think it might be like writing," Hernando said.

"It's exactly like writing," Pizarro replied. "And if Manco is telling the truth, then this is one of many messages from Atahualpa to his generals, summoning them to rescue him."

A murmur of shock went around the room. Juan and the friar, unlikely companions in every other respect, both crossed themselves. DeSoto went to the doorway, twitched aside the curtain and peered out into the darkness, weapon at the ready.

"But Atahualpa gave us his word," Hernando said, frowning.

"He would not be the first to break it," Pizarro asked. "The question is, who do we trust — the Emperor or Manco?"

"Atahualpa is a man of honor," Hernando said.

"Men of honor do dishonorable things when there is a larger cause at stake." Pizarro looked up at his brother — so innocent, by the standards of their group, and yet his knowledge of the Incas made him the best source of insight into this. "Sometimes men pretend to be honorable to get by. And who knows what counts as honor in this land."

He stared expectantly at Hernando, who looked down at the string.

"I don't know," Hernando said at last, his voice flat and empty of emotion. "I'm sorry, but I just don't."

"Anyone else?" Pizarro looked around the room.

"Kill them both," Gonzalo said. "Seize the throne for God and Spain."

Juan grunted his agreement.

"The Emperor has behaved differently since I returned from Cuzco," DeSoto said, stroking his chin thoughtfully. "More friendly. Until now, I thought it was a sign that he had finally learnt some civility. Perhaps it was all a trick."

"He asked to see my Bible," Friar Vicente held out the book. "I hoped that he was turning to the Lord, yet he still carried out his heathen prayers."

"Kill them both and take the throne," Gonzalo said impatiently. "Let's put our blades to use."

"No." Pizarro shook his head. "We need an emperor to control these generals and prevent a rebellion. At the moment, Atahualpa is that emperor. Manco says that if we execute Atahualpa and put him on the throne, he will be our man, and more loyal than the one we have now. So it comes to this — which one do we choose?"

He looked at Hernando, who still stared at the string.

"Kill Atahualpa," Juan said, an excited twinkle in his eyes. "Prove who's in charge."

"Agreed." Gonzalo said.

"We can't just kill him," Hernando said, shocked. "He's our ally."

"No he isn't." The friar shook his head. "He's a heathen who disrespects God with his lies. Better to purge their empire with the sword than doom them all to hell as sinners."

"So we should just kill him?" Hernando said.

The friar hesitated, then shook his head. "Seize him and question him. See where that takes us."

Pizarro watched the flicker of Hernando's eyes as he looked around, deciding what to do. He pitied his brother's softness, a gentleness of spirit that could not stand in times like these.

"Maybe captivity," Hernando said. "Take them both, and try to find out what is happening."

"Better to act decisively," DeSoto said. "Anything else would be a sign of weakness, and we can't afford that."

"On that I agree," Pizarro said. "Better to make a bold mistake than to give the enemy time to act."

"But we don't know who the enemy is!" There was pleading in Hernando's voice.

"Then that isn't how we decide." DeSoto shrugged. "Manco is young and inexperienced, he will be easier to control."

"Please." Hernando turned his gaze fully on Pizarro. "We've built a relationship with Atahualpa. We don't know this Manco. Don't throw away what we have built here."

The decision weighed heavily on Pizarro, but he could not let it bear him down.

"Whatever I decide, I need you all to back me," he said, looking around the room. "Without that, we're all dead."

They nodded their agreement.

"Once we leave this room, there can be no more dissent." Again he looked around. Again they nodded, even Hernando, on whom Pizarro's gaze settled. "Then it is time for me to decide — which of these two barbarians do I trust least?"

CHAPTER TWENTY-NINE

Cajamarca

The sound of rushing footsteps woke Cuyoc. She pulled away her blanket and rubbed her eyes. It was still dark out, the sky beyond the window midnight black rather than the grey that precedes dawn. Stars glittered like tiny campfires across the heavens.

She looked across the room, ready to wake Atahualpa, then remembered that she was not in his prison hut. With their messages on the way and the army assembling, he had wanted her elsewhere. An influx of messengers to her would draw less attention than if they came straight to him. Staying in a small room at the edge of town, she was to be his conduit for what followed.

Something rumbled, and she rose from her pile of cushions to look out. It could not be thunder — there were no clouds in the sky. Instead she saw half a dozen Spaniards pushing one of their cannons down the street to the edge of town, where it would point down the hillside at anyone who approached.

Something was wrong. That much was clear. Looking up at the moon, she prayed to Mama Killa, the goddess of that shining white disk, to protect those who mattered to her —

Atahualpa, Manco, people back at camp. Even Hernando Pizarro.

Hernando. That was how she could find out what was going on. Pulling the cloak tight about her, she hurried out of the hut and through shadowy side streets toward the center of town. This was not a night to be seen.

The Spanish barracks were empty, their inhabitants bustling around Cajamarca. No sign of Hernando in the square either. More men than usual were guarding the treasure room, blades drawn and round shields held before them.

Skirting the edge of town, she came within sight of Atahualpa's prison room. A concentration of Spanish guards was there, weapons drawn, staring out of a ring of bright torches into the night. Among them, she saw Hernando.

She could not risk surprising him, not with everyone on edge. Instead she stepped out into the light and approached carefully. The guards looked at her warily, but Hernando's face filled with relief. He rushed over, sliding his sword back into its scabbard, and leaned in close.

"I was..." He waved his hands in the air, trying to find a word they had never yet used. She nodded her understanding — his expression told her everything she needed to know. Hernando had been worried for her.

"What is happening?" she asked in their hodgepodge private tongue.

He looked over his shoulder at the prison room, then back at her again.

"You don't know?" he said.

She shook her head.

"I..." The words faltered on his lips and he looked away. "I can't tell you."

"You can't tell me what you thought I might know?" She grabbed his arm. "Hernando, what is this?"

"Go find somewhere safe," he said. "A dark room. Up a tree. Some place you won't be seen."

"Do not tell me what to do," she said. "I am a princess and royal councilor."

"That is not a thing to be tonight." He took the hand she had laid on his arm, his fingers gripping tightly around hers.

For the first time since she woke, she felt a fleeting sensation of safety. As his grip on her loosened their fingers intertwined, and he said a word she did not understand. There was a sad look in his eyes as he let go.

"Go." He nodded into the darkness, then turned on his heel and strode back to the guards.

Hernando could not help her. Atahualpa could not be reached. There was only one more person in Cajamarca that night to whom she could turn.

Stealth gave way to haste. Feet slapping against the ground, Cuyoc ran to the house where Manco and his entourage slept. More Spanish guards stood sentinel, hammering her heart with dread. Then, she saw that there was an Inca outside too, and as he turned she saw Manco's face.

"Manco!" She rushed forward, and though the guards glared none tried to stop an unarmed woman. She flung her arms around her younger brother. "Thank the Apus and all their mountains, you are safe."

She took a step back, holding him at arm's length as she had when he was young and she inspected him during visits to court, joking about how much he had grown. He had done all his growing now, in height at least, but to her eyes, he was still the boy she had known.

The boy smiled back at her.

"I hoped to see you, sister," he said. "I have finally learnt from what I saw of you at court. I think you will be proud." His eyes narrowed, sending a chill down her spine. "Though I think you may be upset as well."

"What have you done?" she said, looking around at the Spanish soldiers. She was suddenly aware of how vulnerable she was, unarmed among these fighting men.

"I told Pizarro about what you and Atahualpa were planning," Manco said. "He can't read the quipu, but he took my word for what it meant."

"What quipu?" Cuyoc asked, looking for room to maneuver, some doubt or desire among others with which she could take control.

"Don't play the fool," Manco said. "I saw you gathering your strings. I have one of your messages, and its bearer told me you placed it in his hands."

"How do you know this?"

"For that, Huascar would be proud. Blood spilt in his name. There is more to follow."

Cuyoc took a step back, but one of the Spaniards was blocking her way. He grabbed her arms, fingers digging into her flesh. The pain was nothing next to the dread she felt staring at Manco — this vision of corrupted innocence.

"Did you think that I would leave his death unavenged?" Manco said. "That Atahualpa's bloodlust could be allowed to stand? See how the gods punish us for what he has done, bringing a plague of Spaniards upon our lands. Humiliation at the hands of a dozen foreigners. But now I will turn that plague into a blessing."

Cuyoc watched in shock as the innocent youth she had known turned into a vision of hate. Seeing her expression, he gave a bitter laugh.

"The Spaniards know all about Atahualpa's treachery," he said. "Once he is gone, I will be emperor."

"Please," Cuyoc said, "don't do this. Don't let them tear our people apart."

"We were torn apart long before the Spaniards came," Manco said. He reached out and stroked her cheek with the tips of his fingers. "But do not worry, wise sister. You saved me, and I shall save you. There is a place for you at my court once this is done, but for now I am afraid you cannot be left to roam alone."

He signaled to the guard behind her. Strong hands lifted her from the ground and carried her, kicking and yelling, into the darkness of the hut.

CHAPTER THIRTY

Cajamarca

A woman screamed in the distance. Atahualpa could just make out her voice, but he could not catch the words, only a sound of desperation and anger.

He stood in the center of the house that had become his prison cell. His feathered crown lay on the floor beside him. Slowly he went through the seven fundamental attacks he had learnt as a child, an imaginary axe swinging in his hand. Then the seven basic blocks, each one mirroring one of the strikes. When he reached the end, he went back to the beginning, faster this time, varying the order but always following the same fourteen movements as he swayed in the center of the room. Sweat dappled his skin as he worked himself up into a flurry of attack and riposte. The feeling of warfare, even imaginary warfare, helped to ground him, to drive away the thunderclouds gathering in his mind. He was not some feeble peasant waiting for others to decide his fate. He was a caged animal, looking for its moment to break free.

But he was losing stamina. Though he had exercised every day he was here, still he grew wearier with each passing night. It was a weariness felt in the body but that seemed to originate in the depths of his soul, as if the fire that once burned there had been extinguished. All that remained of the proud war leader was smoke and ashes, memories of the man he had once been.

Before long the will to move left him. He let his arms hang by his sides and stood staring at the curtained doorway. Outside it was still night, the darkness filled with unease. The Spanish had come a few hours before, taken away the servants who waited to tend on him in the night, and carried off most of his possessions. One of them, the man with the crooked nose called DeSoto, had taken special care to gather up the quipu strings Atahualpa kept beneath his cushion bed.

Those cushions were all he had left now, aside from his clothes and his crown. Trying to sleep made the emptiness inside him worse, so he stood and practiced the motions of a warrior.

Footsteps approached. Outside, he heard the guards shuffle to attention. Pizarro swept aside the curtain and strode inside, flanked by the grinning Juan and red-faced Gonzalo, each holding a burning brand that filled the room with sudden light. All wore their armor and weapons. Behind them stood one of their young interpreters and Friar Vicente.

Pizarro flung something upon the ground and stood staring at Atahualpa. The Emperor looked down at the tangle of quipus he had tied.

He knew he had given himself away. During the first fleeting moment, his exhausted mind could not control his reaction. Shock and fear spilt across his face for only a second, but that was long enough.

Pizzaro spoke and the translator turned the message into

words Atahualpa could understand.

"Governor Pizarro says that he knows," the youth said. "Knows you plan fight Spanish."

The impulse to beg for mercy was strong in Atahualpa. Then he remembered Huascar kneeling before him, a pitiful figure trying to escape the fate he had earned.

Atahualpa did not know what he deserved, but whatever it was, he would face it with more pride than his brother had. So he said nothing.

Vicente spoke in Spanish, waving his book with its lopsided cross.

"Friar says he you make good with God," the translator said. "Save soul."

"I care not for your god," Atahualpa said. "I am the blinding light of Inti, he who burns in the sky. I am the voice of Illapa, who is thunder and lightning. I am the strength of the Apus, who endure like their mountains. They will be here long after your god is forgotten, and my soul will rest here with them."

He picked up the crown, its weight enormous to his weary arms, and placed it on his head. There was no point in resisting as Juan and Gonzalo grabbed him by the arms and dragged him toward the door, but this much resistance he could offer — that he walked out of his prison with his head held high.

∽

The sun was rising over the mountains as Cuyoc came into the square, dragged there by one of the Spaniards. Everyone in the terrible drama of the preceding months was here. All the Spaniards. All the servants. Those few nobles who, like her, had stayed in Cajamarca to provide the Emperor with guidance and company. Even the laborers and llama herders who had brought the gold and carried out construction work for the occupiers. They whispered to each other, their voices like the rustle of dying leaves.

Some of the Spanish sat atop their mounts, the beasts snorting and stamping their hooves against the stones. All were armed and armored, swords drawn, harquebuses ready, eyes wandering across the native crowd. Some held themselves with stone-still menace, while others shifted with nerves from foot to foot.

Cuyoc heard loud voices arise from the far end of the square. The crowd parted and Atahualpa emerged, standing proud in his headdress, a patterned tunic in blue and white with the royal red fringe hanging past his knees. Gonzalo and Juan Pizarro, the two most ghastly men she had ever met, gripped him by both arms. The sight froze her thoughts, caught between the knowledge of what must come and the desperate desire to prevent it. She wished she had some gold left, just the slightest token of the gods, so that they might hear her prayers for rescue.

Then came an even more dreadful figure. Francisco Pizarro's expression was as hard as the mountains and looked like the bite of a whip. He strode out into the square behind his brothers and Atahualpa.

Hernando hurried over to him, gesticulating at the Emperor in a way that would be unacceptable at court. Were the world not turned on its head, Hernando would have lost his hands for infringing upon the divinity of the ruler of the

Incas. Yet Cuyoc found no offence in this, only hope. Perhaps Hernando could reason with his brother, showing him how they had left Atahualpa with no choice. Perhaps the situation could yet be saved. Even without gold or fire to guide her prayers she whispered them, hoping that the gods would hear her and lend Hernando's voice their strength.

The Spaniard's voice drifted across the square. She could not catch the words, but their existence gave her comfort. She watched, her heart stirring, as his face filled with passion.

Pizarro cut him off.

"It is decided," the commander said. "Save your strength."

For a moment, Cuyoc let herself hope that Hernando was as good a man as he could be. That he would intervene physically to stop the mistreatment of her brother, of the divine ruler of the Incas. But he stepped back, squaring his shoulders as he joined the other armed Spaniards around the edges of the square.

Part of her mind told her that she had no right to feel betrayed. No agreement existed between her and Hernando, nothing more than tender voices and shared moments. Even if he had been her husband, she could not have expected him to fight his brother in defense of hers. Yet the disappointment was crushing. Everyone had failed her.

Juan and Gonzalo stepped away from Atahualpa. He stood in the middle of that open space, the light of dawn illuminating the feathers of his headdress, turning them the golden orange of a warm fire in winter. He looked into her eyes, and she could not look away. With silent dignity, the Emperor of the Incas faced the crowd.

Pizarro stepped up behind Atahualpa, reached around

and, with a brutal jerk, wrenched a knife across his throat.

Fighting down a scream, Cuyoc kept her eyes locked on her brother's as he sank to his knees, blood streaming from his neck. His face went blank and he fell to one side, pressing against the well-cut stones in a pool of his own blood.

Taking a cloth from his belt, Pizarro wiped the gore from his blade and sheathed it. Then he stooped and picked up Atahualpa's royal headdress. The feathers stained and the gold smeared with blood. More dripped to the floor as he held it out toward someone in the crowd.

The only sounds Cuyoc could hear were the hammering of her heart and the cries of a caracara circling overhead. She watched as Manco stepped out into the square, tripping over a paving stone in his eagerness to take his prize. He was not halfway to Pizarro when the Spaniard tossed the crown to him. Red dots spattered Manco as he caught the headdress and stared down at its feathers, his smile wide with triumph.

As the new Emperor of the Incas turned to face his people, Cuyoc turned her gaze from her living brother to the one she had just lost, his body abandoned in the center of the square. She wanted to cry out in grief, to swear terrible vengeance against those who had caused this.

But vengeance was for the likes of Manco, grief for aging widows, and Cuyoc had no time for either. She had watched her father die of a terrible disease, had seen Huascar butchered on the battlefield, and she had not let herself wallow then. Now, more than ever, she needed to set her emotions aside. One day, she might let out the sea of tears welling up inside her, but now she had a duty to herself, her people, and her family. To the gods and to the world they had put her in.

That once simple duty became harder with each passing moment, not just for her, but for all of those here.

It was the duty to survive.

PART THREE

CHAPTER THIRTY-ONE

Cajamarca Town Square

Pizarro ran the tip of his boot through blood in the center of the town square. It was almost dry, leaving a chalk of dark residue on his toes. A reminder of the man he had tried to work with, and whom he had punished for betrayal. The wasted opportunity annoyed him. He tried to tell himself that was the only reason a thread of regret had knotted around his heart, but that lie was unconvincing even to him.

Would he have done the same as Atahualpa, if he had been in his shoes? Perhaps. But he would have done it better. He would not have been caught.

A disdainful sneer touched his lips. So much for the warrior god the Incas had believed their Emperor to be. What sort of god let himself become trapped as Atahualpa had? What sort of god gave away all his wealth for survival, only to lose his life through poor planning and untrustworthy lieutenants? What sort of god could be killed by a handful of adventurers?

He didn't know what was more pathetic — Atahualpa's weak character or the faith his people had placed in him.

Late morning sunlight poured down upon him. He was

sweltering in his breastplate and helmet. The steel soaked up the warmth of the sun's rays and baked him in it. The padded layers that kept his armor from chafing made the heat even worse. But he would not be removing them today. Perhaps not for the next few days — it would not be the first time he had slept in armor.

Few natives roamed the streets. Those who passed him did so at a distance, hurrying past with their gazes averted. Their eyes might have shifted toward the center of the square, but they looked away in fear the moment they saw him there.

Good. Let them fear him. Let them stew in that fear, until it stained their souls, forever suppressing the possibility of defiance. If this was what it took to show these people what was in their best interests, so be it.

He was not so naive as to believe that with one stroke of the knife he had brought all resistance to an end. Some men respond to violence with anger, not fear. Those were the sort of men he wanted on his side. If they were not, they must be crushed. He looked forward to the fight that would follow, to bringing the rest of these people to heel.

Spurs jangled as DeSoto swaggered across the square, thumbs thrust through his belt. He looked around with the exaggerated slowness of a man trying to hide frayed nerves.

"They're like a hive of bees down there," he said as he reached Pizarro. He nodded toward the edge of town and the valley beyond. "All buzzing and fluttering about since the loss of their queen."

"Let them buzz," Pizarro said. "When they get ready to sting, then I'll care."

"About that..." DeSoto involuntarily looked down to break

his leader's unwavering stare. "I wondered if now might be a good time for you to send someone to Diego. If those stingers come pouring out of their nest, then we will need all the men we can get."

Pizarro had been expecting this. DeSoto was bound to take this opportunity to seek advantage for himself, Diego de Almagro, and whatever troops Almagro had recruited in Panama. What advantage he sought would depend upon how he viewed the current situation. Did DeSoto want Almagro here to make the most of a golden opportunity, or did he want to rush away like a pig fleeing a burning barn?

"You're right," Pizarro said. "Any extra men we can get would be an advantage. Have you thought about who should go to fetch them?"

"I thought I might go myself." DeSoto again looked down as he spoke. "I'm a fast rider, and I know the places Diego is likely to lodge. The sooner we get word to him, the sooner we get help."

So he was the pig after all.

"You make a good point," Pizarro said, fighting back a malicious grin. "And the sooner the message leaves, the sooner it will reach him."

"Exactly. With your permission, I will fetch the fastest horse we have and make it ready."

"Of course," Pizarro said.

DeSoto swept off his helmet in a bow. His spurs jingled as he strode away. He was halfway across the square before Pizarro called out after him.

"Oh, and DeSoto."

"Yes, my lord?" The man turned to face him.

"Put my brother Hernando's saddle on that horse."

"Hernando's?" DeSoto stiffened, his posture a pale imitation of the relaxed figure he had projected. "Surely I will be better off with my own? I've got the stirrups just right for-"

"I couldn't possibly let you go."

Pizarro walked over to DeSoto. The other man's eyes darted back and forth as his commander wrapped an arm around his shoulders and dragged him toward the edge of the town square. Down the street, they had a view into the valley, where the natives were stirring somewhere beyond the trees.

"Think of how that would look," Pizarro said. "If I send away Almagro's right-hand man just as we have collected all this gold. How could he be certain that I wasn't hiding some of it away, to rob him of his rightful share? That I wasn't making power plays that could give me a whole kingdom to rule and leave him with nothing? True, it would be a kingdom full of godless savages, but they are very rich savages.

"Besides, I need my best fighters and my best horsemen here, in case anything goes wrong. No, I cannot possibly spare you at a time like this, my friend."

He squeezed DeSoto's shoulders just a little too tightly, and then let go. Taking a step back, he discarded the air of geniality and let DeSoto see his true face — calm, calculating, and certain.

"Do we understand each other?" he said.

With a deep sigh, DeSoto nodded his head.

"Of course, my lord," he said. "If I am not to ride, what would you have me do now?"

"Why, prepare Hernando's horse, of course," Pizarro said. "As you so kindly offered."

"Of course." DeSoto bowed once more and scurried away. Pizarro smiled to himself. That felt good.

His smile faded as he turned to look down into the valley. He had averted disaster at Atahualpa's hands, but more trouble was coming from the locals. Time would tell whether it came from his own men too.

In the street behind him, two voices raised — Spaniards arguing over some portion of the spoils. Gritting his teeth, Pizarro turned around and strode toward the noise.

CHAPTER THIRTY-TWO

Conquistador Barracks, Cajamarca

Hernando stared at the pile of supplies in the corner of the room. Most were in rough sacks or soft baskets woven out of local fronds. A few carcasses hung from the wall, prizes taken on hunting trips. He doubted anyone from the expedition would be hunting in the next few days while they waited to see what happened next.

Packing up his own possessions for the journey had been easy enough. He knew what he needed, and even while they were here he'd slept with his bag packed, ready to go if Francisco called upon him. But food was another matter. He needed supplies that were light so that he could move quickly. He needed enough to get him to Panama, and to wherever Almagro was. Anything he took deprived his comrades of supplies they might need if the Incas stopped providing them with food — if their loyalty to Manco proved weaker than to Atahualpa.

This was one aspect of the mission he could control, and he had to get it right, not just for his own sake but for that of his confederates.

There were still some dried beans and meat left from their

trek from the coast. Those would be ideal for his journey. He wouldn't take fresh meat — too bulky and would spoil. That could stay here to feed the others. The same went for the dozens of different types of potatoes the Incas had been providing. The first time he tried those strange roots he had found the texture strange and the taste unsatisfying. Over the months in the Americas he had gotten used to them — they were filling, and some of them were even interesting. But their bulk would get in the way on a journey.

He grabbed a sack and filled it.

"So it's true." Friar Vicente appeared in the doorway, staring in at Hernando. "He's sending you to take the message."

"Yes," Hernando said, not keen to talk about it further. He had his opinions, but also had no desire to undermine Francisco. Opinions mattered out here. Morale mattered. Loyalty mattered.

"Idiocy." Vicente threw his arms in the air. "Does he really think he can manage these people while surrounded by Juan and Gonzalo?"

"I would have thought you would be happy to give Juan more prominence," Hernando said. "No one here believes more deeply in God than him."

"A man can be a soldier of Christ and yet remain a hot-headed thug." Vicente slammed his Bible down on the rickety table. "Don't go. Without you here to balance them, this whole expedition will turn into a bloodbath. Juan is eager to do God's work among these heathens, but he makes no distinction between those who may be converted and those who must be slain. And as for Gonzalo…" The friar frowned. "I hear dark things about what happens to the girls in their hut."

Shaking his head, Hernando kept on packing. He hadn't the heart to tell the friar that those dark things were more likely Juan's work than Gonzalo's. Gonzalo liked to keep his bloodshed to the battlefield.

"I'm going," he said. "Francisco has ordered it."

"Then reason with him!" the friar said. "Argue with him. Do whatever it takes. Anyone here can carry a message, but only you can provide a voice of reason."

"I'm flattered by your faith in me, Father," Hernando said. "But the answer is still no."

"Think of these people," Vicente said. "Think of Francisco. Think of your fellow Christian soldiers and what happens to them if things go wrong. Think of Cuyoc, if that's what it takes to move you."

"For the last time no!"

Hernando slammed his fist into the table. A sack fell off, scattering dried kidney beans across the floor. The friar took a step back, staring.

Shocked at the sudden explosion of his own passions, Hernando took a deep, calming breath.

"I apologize, holy Father," he said, stooping to gather up the beans. "As you know, we are all under a great deal of strain, and that is why I must go. Because Francisco is under that strain, and I cannot add to his burden by arguing with him.

"I am not saying that you are wrong. There are times when my brothers are like demons let loose from Lucifer's own house. They slaughter without thought and laugh while doing it. They are far from good men, and as you say, it is all

I can do to balance them in Francisco's councils.

"But just because they do wrong, that does not excuse me from doing right. There are values beyond faith and righteousness, lust and greed. There is loyalty, the ability to stand by our kin, our comrades, and our masters. The willingness to obey when it is needed, to serve not for what we receive in heaven or in a treasure chest, but for the certainty that we can be counted upon, that we are better for our actions, whatever they might be."

Having scooped the last of the beans back into their sack, he added a chunk of dried meat, then carried this and another sack over to his mattress. He placed them beside his bag, then went to the head of the mattress and retrieved something hidden there — a band of grasses and dried flowers with a few long hairs running through it. A keepsake made for him by Cuyoc, a reminder of their days sitting in sunshine on the hillside. Smiling, he slid it into his bag, then turned to face Vicente.

"I understand," the friar said. "But still..."

"Know why I am kinder than my brothers?" Hernando asked. "Because I did not suffer as long as them. Because Francisco came to me when I was a child, and he rescued me from the poverty that had ground him down, that had made Juan and Gonzalo such bitter, broken men. We had never met. We did not share a father. Our mother abandoned him for the new family of which I was a part. And yet, still, he came for me.

"That is loyalty. And now, in a world that threatens to devour us alive, I owe him nothing less."

He placed a hand on Vicente's shoulder.

"You are not wrong in seeing the problems you do, Father," he said. "But sometimes, being right is not enough."

CHAPTER THIRTY-THREE

The Captives' Quarters, Cajamarca

The floor was cold beneath Cuyoc. The whole room was cold, a chill deeper than any she remembered feeling. The sunlight that blazed outside was not warming the air in here. Bright Inti himself mourned the loss of his voice in the world.

Cuyoc pressed herself back into the corner of the room, staring at the pile of cushions on which Atahualpa had slept a day before. Only here, only now, would she let herself be vulnerable. Once she rose from this spot, then she had to be strong. She had to put this behind her and look after her people. Her life depended on it.

However many times she thought it, she could not force herself to her feet.

There was a movement in the doorway. A silhouette stepped forward and became Manco, the feathered crown in his hands. He had wiped away the blood, at least.

"I suppose this will do until I reach my palace," he said. "It will show strength and continuity for me to stay here. As well as saving me from making demands of the Spaniards — no sense in using up any of the goodwill yet."

He placed the crown carefully on a cushion, then stood

over Cuyoc. It was more than she could bear. At last, the pressure of her younger brother's power forced her to her feet, not in obedience to his status, however things might appear, but in silent defiance of it.

"I have a task for you," he said.

Trying to remain calm, Cuyoc gritted her teeth. Part of her wanted to denounce him for what he had done. To slap him across the face and scream at him for his treachery. He had not murdered Atahualpa with his own hands, which only made the act more reprehensible — a piece of cowardice exacerbated by treachery.

But defying him now would do no good. He was the emperor, and she his servant and sister. Silently, she prayed that he would never go further and make her his wife. She thanked the gods they had half-sisters younger and prettier than her.

For the good of the empire, threatened as it was by the Spaniards, it was best that she help the emperor, whoever that might be. For her own safety, it was best that she cooperate with the brother who had already ensured one sibling's death.

"What do you want from me?" she asked.

"The Spaniards are sending a messenger north," Manco said. "One of their own, going to fetch reinforcements. I want you to go with him."

It was a moment's thought to work out why he wanted this.

"You desire intelligence on the Spanish," she said. "Information about what else they have, what else they do, what further monsters and strange weapons they might bring against us."

"Always so smart," Manco said. "I will be sorry not to have you here for advice, but I think you need time to move past last night's events. And there is no one better suited to understand and analyze what you see."

"No," she said. "I will not go. I will not ride with one of these savages to fetch more of their brutal kind. I will not leave this place behind at this time of madness."

"Not even if you were going with Hernando?" Manco asked. "There's something about his eyes, isn't there, that makes him even more handsome than he should be. Were I inclined toward the company of men then I would be very tempted by his."

She stared at her brother, shocked to hear him talking in such a way.

"My mind has not been filled with the arts of war like Huascar and Atahualpa," Manco said. "I have learnt to study and appreciate beauty.

"Now, prepare yourself to travel," Manco said.

"No," she said again. "I want no part of this."

Glancing at the pile of sleeping cushions, she thought again of Atahualpa, of his blood spilling across the square. A shiver of fear ran through her. If that could happen here, who knew what might happen on the road.

Another silhouette filled the doorway. Francisco Pizarro stepped inside, followed by Hernando. The younger Spaniard smiled at her briefly, then grew more serious as he saw how Manco had her pinned into the corner. His hand settled on the hilt of his sword.

"Tell them what we were discussing," Manco said, stepping back a little.

An opportunity opened up before Cuyoc. It should not be hard to get Pizarro to ban her from going.

"My brother the Emperor has a request," she said, pausing for a moment to gather the Spanish she needed to be understood by them. "He wants me to go with Hernando. To see how your Spanish live. To learn more about you."

"A spy," Pizarro said, stroking his beard. Cuyoc hid her satisfaction behind a scowl. "But a guide as well. And a better translator than most. Yes, I think you would be useful."

"No!" she said. "No, I will not go."

Pizarro gave a harsh laugh.

"I command," he said, pointing at himself and then at Manco. "He requests. You obey."

Cuyoc turned a pleading look upon Hernando. He would understand the dangers of this journey, and why she could not agree to help the Spaniards in this — even though he was one of them. He had sway over his brother. Surely he could help.

"Could we have a moment alone?" Hernando asked.

"If it makes this happen quicker," Pizarro said. "Of course." He pointed at Manco and then at the door. "Out."

As their lords left the room, Hernando walked over to Cuyoc. He rested his hands on her shoulders and looked deep into her eyes. The trembling of fear and rage subsided, and at last she felt some calm.

"I understand," he said in their private mixture of Spanish and Incan words. "I understand why you want to stay. But you should come with me."

"What?" She jerked away from his touch.

"While you are with me, I can protect you," Hernando said. "But I have to go, and we do not know what will happen here next. So please, come with me. I could not bear the thought of leaving you in danger."

"But my people..." she said, her resistance starting to melt.

"I will return you to them," he said. "In a few weeks' time you will be back."

"You cannot promise this," she said. "Travel is dangerous. Spaniards are dangerous. We would travel to a nest of them."

"I promise," Hernando said, taking her hand and sinking to his knees. "I promise, as long as there is breath in my body, I will keep you safe."

Cuyoc's body trembled, but no longer in anger or fear.

"I will come," she said.

CHAPTER THIRTY-FOUR

Francisco Pizarro's Lodgings, Cajamarca

Pizarro watched from his rooftop as the Panama-bound party trekked up the hillside. There were less than a dozen of them — Hernando, Cuyoc, and a handful of guards and servants. Enough to deter idle robbers, but would they be enough if serious opponents sought to stop them getting through? If some other conquistador, jealous of the Pizarro brothers' success, sought to stop them linking up with Almagro, could Hernando fight his way through? If a faction of Inca still loyal to Atahualpa wanted Spaniards to attack, would Cuyoc's presence be enough to put them off? If any of the answers were no, his ability to intervene would end when they crossed the ridge and disappeared from sight. Until then, he at least had the chance to tip the scales.

At last, they reached the crest of the ridge, the same spot from which Pizarro had first seen Cajamarca all those weeks before. Hernando turned, just identifiable from the others at this distance, raised his helmet and waved at the town. Then they disappeared from view.

Turning away, Pizarro cast his gaze down into the valley. There was nothing he could do for Hernando now except pray, and that could wait until dark. For now, he had other matters to attend to.

"Gonzalo!" he said.

The ladder creaked as his brother ascended, then stepped onto the roof. He looked with distaste at the black and white stains that dappled the thatch.

"Do those damn buzzards of yours ever stop shitting?" he asked.

"Do you?" Pizarro said. "They are not buzzards. They are caracara."

"Bunch of useless scavengers," Gonzalo said. Then he looked at Pizarro and forced a smile. "I jest, of course. The very fact that you enjoy their company is a sure sign that..."

"Save it," Pizarro said. "Turn what thoughts you have to the valley instead. What do you make of the Incan camp?"

Gonzalo stood beside Pizarro, a pair of gargoyles staring down from the top of the building. Both muscled and scarred, their better features wearing down with age, their leggings patched and their armor dented. Pizarro believed that his family had fine features, but aside from Hernando none of them could ever be said to be beautiful.

"There are less of those heathen bastards, aren't there?" Gonzalo said. "It's not obvious at first, what with all the shelters and fire pits they've left behind. But there aren't half as many people moving around as before."

"And what does that tell us?" Pizarro asked.

"That there's loot to be had." Gonzalo grinned. "I'll gather the boys together and we can..."

"No." Pizarro held up a hand. "Again, use your thoughts, not your greed. Do you really think they brought anything of value within our reach without using it to buy Atahualpa's way out? Or that they would leave gold in abandoned bivouacs? These are savages, not bloody faeries leaving treasures for adventurers. So, think again, what does this mean?"

Gonzalo's ugly scowl turned to a contemplative expression as he studied the valley below. At last, realization dawned.

"It means they've taken soldiers elsewhere," he said. "Either Manco's taken them out of our reach, or they're not obeying him anymore. Either way, someone's gathering an army elsewhere."

"Well done." Pizarro said. "I need you to practice using your mind like this, Gonzalo. If anything happens to me, I want one of my brothers taking over. If Hernando is here, that means you back him up. If not, then it's you. I won't let all we've worked toward slip into someone else's hands. Do you understand?"

"You think Hernando could do better than me?" Gonzalo said.

"For now, yes. He thinks more. But he lacks your effectiveness. So practice thinking, understand?"

"Yes, Francisco." Gonzalo grinned. "Thank you, brother."

"Now come, we need to talk with our pet Emperor."

They descended the ladder and strode through the streets toward the captives' quarters. At a shout from Pizarro, one of the translators hurried to join them, the youth scampering in Gonzalo's wake.

Manco was not sitting inside the room he had been assigned, as his brother had. Instead, he sat on a cushion down the dirt track from there, shaded by a tree at the edge of town. His was one of a circle of cushions, each with an adviser sitting upon it. Around them, armed Spanish guards watched for any sign of rebellion, either among their captives or emerging from the shadows of the nearby jungle.

None of the natives stood as Pizarro arrived, but taking their cue from Manco, they bowed their heads enough to show respect, without subservience.

Pizarro narrowed his gaze. This was no simple youth he had helped to the throne. There was a sharp mind hiding behind those soft features.

Looking around the circle, he was surprised at what he saw. He had expected that Manco would raise his peers to positions of status, assembling a council as young as he was. Instead, these were old men, their faces crumpled and their hair turning to grey. Something was at play that he did not understand. That was not a feeling he liked. He would have to work out what this meant, but for now other matters came first.

"Many soldiers have gone from the valley," he said. "What is happening?"

He kept his eyes on Manco as the translator turned his words into the Incan language and Manco responded.

"He says he does not know," the translator said. "But he suspects that they have turned their backs on him. Either they have scattered to seize lands for themselves, or they are planning some act of revolt."

"How do I know this is not some scheme of his?" Pizarro said, pointing at Manco.

The Emperor nodded and smiled, unfazed by the accusation, as the translator spoke.

"He says that you gave him power," the translator said,

"and he intends to keep it. I think he is saying that he can gather other armies... Yes, generals who fought for his brother Huascar against Atahualpa. Men who will side with him. He says that you should march to Cuzco and seize the capital, so that your enemies may not, and so that he may start governing the empire in earnest. He says that, with your permission, he will send to those generals and ask them to meet there."

"He wants to gather an army?" Pizarro hesitated. He never would have trusted Atahualpa with such a plan, but then Atahualpa held power despite the Spaniards, not because of them. If his enemies were gathering an army then he would need one of his own long before Almagro and reinforcements could arrive.

It was a risk. But then this whole expedition was a risk.

"Tell him to send his messengers," he said. "I will prepare my men to march."

The Incas huddled together, talking frantically as they made plans. Pizarro turned to Gonzalo.

"Your second lesson of the day," he said. "Thinking is important, but so is decisiveness. Now go gather our commanders — we have plans to make."

CHAPTER THIRTY-FIVE

Cuzco

Quehuar had never seen so many great men assembled in one place. He had met each one of them with his father, a noble like them, a minor man around court but one who had led men in war. He knew that they had led Atahualpa's armies. He had served under two of them on different campaigns, while he learnt to fight and his father commanded forces elsewhere. But never before had he seen them all together.

And never before had they treated him as a peer.

Here he was, seated in the council chamber of an imperial palace, alongside men who had fought rebels and barbarians, who had brought savage Amazon tribes to heel, expanding the empire with their sweat, blood, and cunning. Some had even survived Cajamarca, bringing back news of the death of his father and so many others, word of the Emperor Atahualpa's capture and everything that had followed. They had looked at him softly when they brought that first news, shock and grief all but overwhelming them. Now their eyes were as hard as stone.

The conversation was done. There had been little dissent among them. Those who disagreed were doubtless with

Manco, the serpent who would be emperor.

Just hearing Manco's name made Quehuar's skin crawl. These strangers from over the mountains had killed Quehuar's father and his brother, leaving him to take their place in court and in war. There could be only one response to outsiders murdering great men, the elite who governed Incan lands, the kin who gave life meaning. That response was death.

Yet instead of defying those strangers, Manco had joined them in perpetrating his own brother's murder. Like Huascar before him, he had defied the will of divine Inti and his messenger upon the earth. Like Huascar, he must be made to pay.

One by one, the generals stepped forward. One by one, they took up the bronze knife that lay on a marble slab in the center of the room. One by one, they ran it across the backs of their hands, each uttering the same oath as their blood joined the pool in the sacrificial bowl.

"Vengeance for Atahualpa. Death to invaders. Life for the empire."

At last, it was Quehuar's turn. Every eye in the room turned toward him. Men with twice his experience and wisdom watched respectfully as he took his place at the slab, the place that should have been his father's. The hands that came before had warmed the handle of the knife. The blade was stained with the blood of better men.

In the silence of his mind, he swore his own oath. This vengeance was not just for Atahualpa, it was for his family too. Running the knife across the back of his hand, he barely felt the pain as blood ran hot across his skin and into the bowl.

"Vengeance for Atahualpa," he said, his words echoing

around the room. "Death to invaders. Life for the empire."

He dropped the blade onto the slab. Everyone had taken the oath. Now they rose from their seats, blood still dripping from unbandaged hands as they walked to the windows and, together, stared out at the plains below Cuzco. Thousands of men gathered to do the will of the gods. Inti's strength in human form.

A mighty army had gathered. Soon there would be war.

∽

"I will admit, this is less stately than our last journey across these hills," DeSoto said, swatting a fly from his sweaty face. "But is there not a certain glory in marching under arms? The bright shining banners. The glory of Christ's gleaming soldiers tramping toward the wretched foe."

He waved back toward the column of followers barging through the jungle. Every man covered in dust. After weeks on the road, their smell stretched half a mile before them. If they had brightly colored banners then they were curled safely away to avoid tangling with the trees. Even the lances of the cavalry were not held high, but strapped to the sides of mules for the duration of the trek.

"You should write this stuff down," Zárate said. "I hear rich people will pay a lot to read fantasies of the imagination."

"Really?"

Zárate shrugged. "I'm a disgraced clerk from a backwater town. How many rich people do you think I've met?"

"All of us." DeSoto waved at the column again. "After all, we have plenty of gold."

"I'm rich and I don't even know how to read," someone

called out from behind them.

"But will we live to spend it?" Zárate asked.

That was the thought DeSoto himself had been avoiding. He hadn't come to the New World because it was a safe thing to do, but this expedition was getting more precarious with each passing day. Supplies were running low, men were falling sick, and they all knew there was a battle coming. He recognized this road from their previous journey to Cuzco, and if the enemy were gathered there then that battle might only be a day away. He loved the idea of being rich, of regaining the aristocratic status his father assured him they had lost. But such status wasn't worth dying for.

As if in response to those dark thoughts, three riders appeared on the road up ahead — the Pizarro brothers, returning from scouting the enemy. And running behind them, still nervous of the horses, a pair of Manco's Incan scouts.

Juan and Gonzalo galloped past DeSoto without a word, barely even acknowledging him. It was the sort of arrogance he'd come to expect from those two. He would happily have left them to be butchered by savages, given half a chance.

Francisco Pizarro dragged his horse to halt and leapt down next to DeSoto. His expression was grim.

"Manco was right," Pizarro said. "There's an army up ahead, and it's far larger than ours."

"Are they on the plains in front of the city?" DeSoto asked.

Pizarro nodded. "You were right. Are you certain there's no way around them?"

"Can a man be certain of anything?" DeSoto asked. "Perhaps we will rise tomorrow to find the sun gone or our weapons turned to frogs in the night. Perhaps we will find a city covered in gold." He paused for effect. "No, wait, I did that last one. So, really, anything could happen in this New World."

"Now is not the time for jokes," Pizarro said. "A great battle is looming, and we need any advantage we can get."

"I'm sorry," DeSoto said, surprised to find that he meant it. It was hard not to respect Francisco Pizarro and his great sense of purpose, however little respect his brothers might earn. "I try not to treat impending doom seriously; it just depresses me. In answer to your question, there are ways around the enemy's flanks, but I don't think we can take them. I didn't explore far beyond the city, as that was where the gold was, but the tracks I saw did not look like easy work. We would become strung out, vulnerable to attack, unable to properly use the guns or the horses."

"In short, we would lose what advantage we have," Pizarro said. "Very well then, we march on, and hope that reinforcements arrive before battle is forced."

"Anything could happen," DeSoto said with a smile that didn't reach Pizarro's eyes. "After all, this is the New World."

CHAPTER THIRTY-SIX

Panama City

If there was a more wretched town on Earth than Panama City, Hernando had not seen it. The place was a heaving mass of humanity at its worst — greedy, filthy, and degenerate — a place of opportunists, broken dreamers, and victims of other men's schemes. Buildings had been flung up with little consideration for beauty or solid construction. The erratic mess looked like one good storm might smash it to kindling and a single match would trigger an inferno.

Of course, it also contained humanity at its maximum incarnation. The boldness of spirit that led men to strange new lands. The ingenuity that let them squeeze treasures out of every land they found, treasures piled up in baskets and barrels along the bustling docks. There were sleek ships with tall masts and sturdy rigging, ready to carry these goods back across the Atlantic, exchange them for new adventurers, and return for the next round.

Yet this pioneering spirit seemed to accentuate the wretchedness, both moral and physical, not to counter it. It brought out what was worst and raised it to the top of a heap, like a rat dragging something rotten to the top of a dung pile.

The inn they were staying in, The Crown, was the best he could find. After all, they had the gold to afford it, and having seen the stricken look on Cuyoc's face, he wanted to save her from the stink and the chaos as best he could. But now he had to go to one of the worst inns in the city.

"I would like to come with you," Cuyoc said as they finished eating breakfast in the inn's main room.

Hernando shook his head. "You stay here. I'll leave the others to look after you."

"I want to see your city," she said. "To understand how people can live like this."

She appeared sincere, despite the twinge of uncertainty as she looked out the window, still struck by shock and awe at the ships on the dock.

"Later," Hernando said. "For now, I have to go to some unpleasant places filled with worse people. You have told me of the gleaming beauty of Cuzco, but now imagine its opposite. As Cuzco is to heaven, these places are to hell. It is a hell full of desperate men and very few women, and I fear that your beauty might inflame them. It will be hard to do business if I am fighting duels to keep you safe."

"So this inn is your treasure room?" she said. "A way to hide beauty from the world?"

"Please." He reached out and squeezed her hand. "Please, this once, just rest. There will time for exploring later."

"Very well," she said with a sigh. "I only hope that your beauty does not inflame these men too."

∽

The inn didn't even have a name, just a broken bottle hanging above its doorway and a stink of cheap wine emanating out on the stale air. Reluctantly, Hernando pushed the door open and stepped into the gloom.

No one looked up as he entered, yet he had the feeling of many gazes surreptitiously turning toward him. There were a surprising number of drinkers for such an early hour.

The bald barman turned to face Hernando, a lumpy jug in one hand and a clay cup in the other.

"You want beer?" he asked, his words Spanish but his accent Portuguese. He looked Hernando up and down with an appraising eye, then set aside the jug and pulled out a grimy bottle. "No, you're clearly a wine man."

"I'm looking for Diego de Almagro," Hernando said.

"Then I hope you've brought enough to pay his bill," the barman said. "And it won't be cheap."

"If that's true then he can pay it himself." Hernando crossed his arms. "Now where is he?"

"There."

The barman pointed to the darkest corner of the room. A man lay slumped across a table, one arm dangling toward a cup dropped in the wood shavings on the floor. His shirt, which had presumably once been white, was dark with wine stains.

Hernando walked over to the corner. Was this really the man of whom Francisco had spoken so highly, with whom he had shared many of his greatest adventures? He looked more like Juan at his worst, passed out in a haze of his own wretchedness.

"Almagro?" Hernando said, lip curling in distaste.

The man did not stir.

"Almagro?" He tapped him on the shoulder. Still no response.

"Diego de Almagro!" Hernando hauled the man up by his collar. Lank hair flopped aside, revealing the ugliest face Hernando had ever seen. It was the Panama City of faces, unshapely and deeply scarred. As the man's eyes opened, one was revealed to be a dead white orb amid a mass of puckered flesh.

"Whah?" Almagro said. "Wha' you want?"

He pulled himself to his feet, wrenched out of Hernando's grip, and staggered back. His head thudded off the wall and he slid to the ground.

Cackles of cruel laughter filled the bar.

Anger welled up in Hernando. Grabbing hold of Almagro once more, he dragged the groaning drunk through the filthy sawdust to the front door.

"His bill!" the barman called out.

"If he's still alive, he'll be back to pay it," Hernando said, dragging him into the street.

There was a water trough across the street, a couple of horses drinking from it. Shouldering the beasts aside, Hernando plunged Almagro headfirst into the water, yanked him out coughing and spluttering, then plunged him in again.

This time Almagro emerged of his own accord. Wriggling free of Hernando's grip, he staggered to the nearest building and leaned against its rough plank walls, water running down his face.

"Who the hell are you?" he said, wiping his eyes. "And why shouldn't I run you through for your insolence?"

"I'm Hernando de Pizarro," Hernando said. "My brother

sent me. And if you think you can win a fight against a toddler right now, then you're a bigger fool than I already take you for."

"Pizarro, eh?" Almagro grinned. "Guess Francisco sent you for his reinforcements."

"He shouldn't have had to send me," Hernando said. "You were meant to send them to Peru months ago. I'm starting to think the only reinforcements you've bought come in a bottle."

"I've found the men," Almagro said, wobbling as he pushed himself away from the wall. "Found the men, all right. Fine men. Upright men. Men of God and blood and honor and blah, blah, blah..."

He burst out laughing.

"Then why aren't they in Peru?" Hernando asked. "We've been fighting for an empire while you're fighting for a table. If Francisco dies because you were too busy drinking to send support, I swear by every saint in the heavens and every star in the sky, I will see you share his fate."

"Calm yourself, young Pizarro," Almagro said, laying a soggy arm around Hernando's shoulders. Rancid breath brushed the younger man's face. "I've just been waiting for ships to carry them south. But if you're here, we can sort that out together."

He waved a hand wildly in the air.

"To the docks!" he exclaimed. "To Peru! To our empire and my good friend Francisco! And little Pizarro?"

"Yes?" Hernando snapped, looking down at the other man.

"I may be drunk, but I'm a damn fine swordsman. Insult

me when I'm sober, and we'll see who shares a dead man's fate."

CHAPTER THIRTY-SEVEN

Panama City

Every part of Hernando felt weary. His legs, from tramping back and forth across Panama City, as a wretched, disorganized Almagro tried to prove what he'd achieved. His back, from leaning over tables in a dozen different taverns and lodging houses, discussing plans and requirements with the men Almagro introduced him to. His head, from trying to keep track of it all, piecing together what Almagro had achieved, counting up the men available to them and the worth of those recruits if it came to a fight.

He had to admit, Almagro hadn't done a bad job. Most of the men were tough, experienced, and far more sober than Almagro himself. Hernando gained an impression of calm competence at almost every turn, and of a respect for Almagro that truly surprised him. Were these men missing something about their employer, or was he? Which was the truth — the shambling drunk or the effective negotiator and veteran explorer?

One thing was clear — Almagro couldn't entirely be trusted. But what other options were there for providing the troops Francisco needed?

Weighed down beneath the burden of it all, Hernando stepped out of the last grey light of dusk and into the warm light of candles and a fire blazing in The Crown's main room.

Cuyoc sat in a corner, along with most of the men who had come with them from Cajamarca. He smiled when he saw, amid the empty cups and plates covering their table, a platter of bread and roasted meat. Sinking onto the empty stool beside Cuyoc, he greeted them all, then set to devouring the food.

"How does it look?" grizzled old Martín asked, pouring Hernando a cup of wine.

Hernando swallowed a large mouthful of bread and washed it down with a gulp of vinegary red. Food and drink had seldom tasted so good. After months in the south, surviving off trail rations and strange local foods, then a day tramping around after Almagro, it was glorious to fill up on good Spanish fare.

Pausing for wine also gave Hernando a moment to reflect. How much should he talk about with these men? Didn't commanders usually use discretion when dealing with difficult situations?

But these men had crossed a continent with him. They had risked their lives for the sake of what his brother had put into action. He would trust any one of them to have his back in battle. Couldn't he trust them now? And shouldn't they be able to trust him to be honest in what was passing?

"It's not all bad," he said, setting aside his plate for a moment. "Everybody he's hired seems competent. They all have their own weapons, and they're all more than happy to come with us. I didn't tell them everything, especially where the gold's concerned, but I let them know what sort of danger they're walking into, and that only put one off.

"The problem's transport. Almagro says he needs gold to pay for shipping down the coast. I'm still not sure how far I trust him. He could have friends among the captains here and a scam in mind. And I don't have any way of assessing if we're getting our money's worth."

"Yes, you do," Martín said, pointing at himself. "I used to be a sailor. Sure, I didn't negotiate big jobs like this, but I overheard captains doing it. I can judge a ship and crew, no problem, and a price if that's what's needed. After all, I'm owed a share of this gold we could end up wasting."

Some of the weariness lifted from Hernando. He snatched a slice of pork from his plate and chewed it with gusto.

"Martín, I could kiss you," he said. "But you're far too pretty for me."

The men all laughed, a servant came with more wine, and Cuyoc leaned in close to talk with Hernando about the things she'd seen that day. For the first time since leaving Cajamarca, he was able to relax.

~

The docks were crowded with men and goods. Conquistadors waiting to embark, laborers hauling in supplies, sailors working around them all. Piles of weapons sat beside barrels of fresh water and sacks of food. There were whetstones, spare gun parts, and a portable anvil, as well as the tools that went with it.

In the center of it all stood Hernando ordering the men about, Cuyoc counting supplies on her strings, and Martín overseeing the nautical side of the business.

"Ship's nearly ready," the old sailor said, pointing to the craft in front of them. "Rigging's good, and we judged the space right for food supplies. The captain got rid of that drunken first mate, and the new man Almagro found isn't bad."

"You could have taken the job," Hernando said. "It might have been your first step toward becoming the new Columbus, parting the waves in your quest to find new worlds and the wonders they hold."

Martín snorted. "I'm a simple sailor and soldier, not one for command. I'll be glad to get back to other people bossing me around. Speaking of which..."

He nodded toward the road, where Almagro was striding toward them, a huge grin splitting his scarred face. They hadn't quite managed to keep all the gold out of his hands, and the bright, blue shirt he now wore was less stained and far better mended than the one Hernando had found him in.

"Young Pizarro!" Almagro exclaimed as he approached. "I need a word with you before we depart."

The older conquistador flung an arm up around Hernando's shoulder and led him away from the others.

"Isn't it amazing?" Almagro said, his breath smelling only a little of wine. "This expedition we have thrown together and the glories it will achieve."

"Amazing indeed, when you consider how it began," Hernando said.

"Don't push me, young Pizarro," Almagro said, his voice suddenly cold. "You may have the money, but these men have known me longer. Who knows which way they will side if we fall out."

"I apologize." Hernando let out a sigh. He didn't even know why he had said what he did. Just being around Almagro brought out an edge in him that he didn't much like. "What did you want to discuss?"

"This empire we are forging, down in the south," Almagro said. "Francisco and I dreamed of it together. It was at his insistence that I came here to recruit instead of travelling with the rest of you. The dream we are unfolding is as much mine as his. The empire we are building as much mine as his."

Hernando stiffened but didn't interrupt.

"I want your word, young Pizarro, as your brother's envoy, that he and I will be joint rulers of that empire. That I will not play second fiddle because mine was the less glamorous job."

"I cannot promise that," Hernando said.

"Remember what I said," Almagro said, squeezing Hernando's shoulders more tightly. "About the men. About their loyalties."

"I mean no insult," Hernando said. He needed to keep this group together, to get Almagro's men down to Francisco and his outnumbered force. It might gall him, but he had to keep this man happy as best he could. "I don't have the authority to make such a promise for my brother, though I am sure he would not object to its substance. How could he, when you two are such firm friends? When you dreamed this dream together?"

"So the empire will be his?" Almagro said.

"That is for you and him to discuss. I am, as you point out, the young Pizarro — last in line to make such big decisions."

Almagro's eyes narrowed, and Hernando slid his hand

around to the hilt of his sword. Then the one-eyed man laughed and slapped him on the back.

"You're pretty smart, you know that?" Almagro said. "Come on then, I've got half an empire to conquer, and that won't get done in Panama."

CHAPTER THIRTY-EIGHT

The Plains of Cuzco

The city of Cuzco was a specter looming over the plain, a ghostly imitation of the cities Pizarro had known in Spain — its shapes paler and cleaner, familiar and foreign at the same time.

Looking up, he expected to see the caracara circling. After all, there were two armies here preparing to fight. Win or lose, his work would feed those birds this evening. And yet the sky was clear, nothing but white clouds against noble blue all the way to heaven. Instead, the caracara perched in the trees at the edge of the plain. Only God looked down from above, ready to judge the dead rather than to feast on them.

And how would he judge them, Pizarro wondered, looking up and down the lines. Here were all the conquistadors who remained, their numbers reduced by disease and the departure of Hernando's party north to Panama. Weeks now without word of progress. He prayed that the jungle had not swallowed up his brother and with him their best hope for victory.

To either side of the Spaniards stood ranks of native troops, most of them in the simply patterned tunics so common in these parts. A few wore layers of padded cotton, like the arming jacket a soldier might wear beneath his armor, except without metal over the top. Such costume might spread the impact of a club or reduce the penetration of a blunt arrow, but it could offer little help against steel and shot.

That was the factor upon which their fates depended. For though nobody on the opposing side was equipped to match the Spaniards, they outnumbered Pizarro and Manco's force at least three to one. Numbers weren't everything — the fighting in Cajamarca had proved that — but if the natives had recovered from the shock of facing European warfare, and if he could not find a way to outmaneuver those superior numbers, then things could go very badly.

"What experience do your men have?" he said, leaning over in the saddle to speak with Manco in his royal litter.

"Very little," Manco replied, by way of the translator placed awkwardly between them. His grim expression needed no translating. "Most of the veterans loyal to Atahualpa were killed along with him or are still on their way here."

"And them?" Pizarro pointed across the plain at the assembled throng. "Are they as useless as what you have provided?"

The translator hesitated as he conveyed the words into the Incan language, and Pizarro had no doubt that the less delicate nuances became lost along the way. Still, Manco squirmed as he responded.

"The Emperor wishes there to be no deceptions between you," the translator began.

"How good of him," Pizarro said. "But please translate my words exactly or I'll have you skewered."

"Many of those men are veterans," the translator said. "Warriors from the army that took the throne for Atahualpa. Some served him for years beforehand in the northern wars."

"Their generals?"

"The finest in the land."

"Then pray to whatever idols you believe in that this land breeds worthless men."

A drumming of hooves announced Juan and Gonzalo's arrival, their tour of the lines complete.

"Well?" Pizarro said.

"As good as it's going to get," Gonzalo said, his expression grim. "DeSoto's taken a few men to anchor the left. We've set the right flank so weakly they should think it's a trap."

"Which it is," Juan said, grinning. "A trap containing cannons to punish a cautious advance."

Juan already had the battle fever in his eyes. A look that on him was not far from lust. Gonzalo, more realistic about what sheer brutality could achieve, set his face to an expression of determination. DeSoto, trudging toward them with an harquebus in one hand and a length of match smoldering in the other, had the hangdog expression of a condemned man.

"I would never lie to you bastards," Pizarro said to his commanders. "This is going to be a bloody business, and unless God looks very kindly on us we may all be forsaken. But it's too late to withdraw now. Their scouts are in the jungle, and it would take hours to leave this field by the way we came — hours with our shrinking forces exposed to the Incas' best.

"So this is it. Pray hard, fight well, and if I don't see you in Cuzco I'll see you in heaven."

He turned to look at Manco, struggling to keep up as the translator tried to make sensible Incan out of Pizarro's words.

"All except him," Pizarro said, tipping his helmet and smiling benignly at the new Emperor. "After all, heathen dogs go to hell."

He watched the translator's eyes go wide and his words come to a hasty halt.

"To your places," Pizarro said. "On my mark, advance."

Two minutes later, they were marching across the plain, guns and swords at the ready, the men on horseback carrying lances. To either side, their Incan allies seemed to swarm forwards rather than march like fighting men, their formations loose and unruly.

Any thought that this was how all Incas fought was quickly dispelled. The opposing army let out a sharp collective shout then began to march, chanting to keep time as they did so. Thousands of scarred, muscled veterans wielding heavy clubs and long-hafted axes.

The very sight struck fear into the Incan irregulars, and the right flank began to crumble. Pizarro cursed under his breath. He needed them farther advanced before that happened, needed to give the cannons more time to fire.

Now the enemy was approaching at double pace, gaining momentum, their chant turning into bloodcurdling screams. Bracing himself, Pizarro muttered one last prayer for his immortal soul and prepared to meet his maker.

A flash of light to the right caught his eye. Blinking, he looked to see what fresh misery the Incas were bringing upon him.

Shining like deadly stars, a thousand armored knights

charged out of the jungle. Above their heads flew two banners — a proud Spanish flag and an old sheet painted with a single eye.

Almagro had arrived.

CHAPTER THIRTY-NINE

The Plains of Cuzco

Quehuar had been afraid when he saw horses in the center of the enemy lines. It was a sight to drive a man mad, these dozen strange beasts with their sleek, muscled flanks, gleaming hooves, and flailing eyes. He joined in the battle chant as much to channel his fear as to keep the rhythm of the advance. Sweat made the handle of the club slippery in his grip.

When he saw a thousand of the monsters charging out of the jungle, each one carrying a gleaming silver man with a twenty-foot spear, that fear transformed into terror and then emerged out the other side of his scream, becoming something he had never felt before. The certainty that death was here, brutal and unstoppable. Recognition that it was futile to resist. Not a decision to stand and fight, but a sense of the inevitability of it.

Manco's forces — these rebels and traitors who would rather fight for foreign devils than for justice against an emperor's murderer; these men who moments before had turned their backs to run — now formed a battle line, screaming in excitement as the demons they summoned galloped toward the righteous.

Raising his shield, Quehuar prayed to Inti and prepared to stand his ground.

∽

As the horses thundered out of the tree line, pride swelled in Pizarro. There was Hernando, his tall figure and handsome face unmistakable even mounted and shaded by a helmet. He had succeeded. He had brought the help they needed.

Beside Pizarro's youngest brother rode his oldest friend, contrasting images of youthful beauty and scarred ugliness. Yet they shared an expression of excitement as they smashed into the Incan flank, driving holes through the loyalist lines.

"With me!" Pizarro yelled to his handful of cavalry, setting the spurs to his horse. Together they plunged toward the center of the enemy formation, its men wavering as they glanced fearfully at the carnage to their left.

The best infantry in the world could not stand against a cavalry charge if they did not maintain their lines. These were far from the best infantry in the world. Gaps appeared before Pizarro and his men. The first Inca with the courage to stand before him was trampled beneath his horse, the next skewered on his lance. Casting that aside, Pizarro drew his sword and hacked at any Inca he passed — cold steel rending padded cloth and warm flesh as he burst through, reached the far side, and turned to gallop in again.

His heart raced and blood spattered his face. He had never felt so alive.

∽

Quehuar cast aside the remains of his mangled shield. All

around him was chaos, men not knowing which way to flee, never mind which way to turn and fight. The screams of the dying were interspersed with the frantic jabbering of terrified survivors.

If they were to rescue this moment then they had to act together, to use their weight of numbers against their enemies' monstrous steeds and silver weapons.

"You, you, you." Quehuar pointed at the three nearest men, singling them out so firmly that instinct took over and they turned to hear his commands. "Pick up the largest shields you can find. Get two more men each to do the same. Then come with me."

It was as if his father's spirit had entered into him, the old war leader acting through the body of the young. To his amazement, the men reacted to him as they had his father, continuing to obey without question. Seeing some semblance of order, others followed, and soon he had twenty men with shields following him toward the thick of the fighting.

Ahead he spied his target — one of the mounted Spaniards. Spreading his men out, he encircled the isolated invader in a wall of shields. The horse reared but his men held firm, chanting prayers to drive back the demon, and closed in, trapping the beast in a smaller and smaller space.

The Spaniard lashed out with his sword, slicing a wicker shield in half, taking the top off another, and caving a man's face in. But now he had no room to maneuver.

This was Quehuar's moment. Mace in hand, he leapt up onto the back of the beast. He feared that its black magic might rise up to engulf him or that its eldritch chill might freeze him to the bone. Instead, it was warm and firm as any muscled beast.

Wrapping his arm around the Spaniard's neck, Quehuar flung him from the horse and leapt down on top of him, smashing his club into the man's raised hand. Quehuar's followers closed in, axes and maces pounding the Spaniard in a deadly frenzy.

∼

"That's the third knight we've lost," Hernando yelled, pointing across the battlefield. There had been too many men for him to get to know them all well on the journey down, but he knew all their faces and most of their names. Every death was a burden he would carry, a man he had led here to die.

Was this how it felt to be a leader like Francisco — to have men's lives dependent on your every decision?

"Three is nothing," Almagro yelled over the sounds of combat. "Haven't you ever been in a battle before, boy? To lose only three in this mess would be a bloody miracle!"

As if to drive his point home, Almagro drove his sword down into the shoulder of an Incan fighter. The man was one of a dozen trying to take on the aging conquistador, held back by the fear of his horse and the fact that their weapons could not penetrate his armor.

"And I do mean bloody," Almagro said.

A blow bounced off Hernando's own breastplate, causing him to turn his attention back to fighting. The conquistadors might be almost indestructible in the face of Incan weapons, but he didn't want to become a victim of "almost."

∼

Bruised and bloody, Quehuar staggered toward the tree line. With every step, he glanced back over his shoulder, fearful that a Spaniard might ride him down and finish him off.

At least the blood wasn't all his, though the broken arm most certainly was. He could feel the bones grinding together, setting his teeth on edge. Who would have thought that the monsters could kick so hard?

Who would have thought he would become so nonchalant about them so quickly? Then that had been his downfall, believing that taking down one Spaniard meant he could take them all. He had been proved wrong when he made his second attempt to drag one from the saddle and was instead nearly trampled to death.

The army was scattered now, Manco and his foul allies having won the day. The calm, confident voice within Quehuar, the one he thought of as his father's spirit, was proud of the fact that he was one of the last. He had done right by his family, that voice said, even if his leaders had failed him and the forces of darkness had become too powerful to defeat.

Twenty feet from the trees, he heard thunder. Looking back, he saw a rider galloping toward him, lance raised, a look of vicious glee on his face.

With his unbroken arm, Quehuar raised his club, ready to channel that spirit one last time.

CHAPTER FORTY

Cuzco

The last time DeSoto had entered Cuzco he had been a different man. Clean, well-rested, his tunic not damp with sweat beneath an armored breastplate. His hair had been carefully arranged, not flattened by the steel and padding of his helmet. He had not stunk of blood, sweat, and powder smoke. His mouth had not been filled with the bitter aftertaste that came as battle passion wore off and his all too frail body began the slow slide toward an exhausted sleep.

Yet he felt grander this time. More powerful, despite not being brought in on a litter. More important, despite being just the gunners' commander instead of the lead delegate of an embassy. More dashing, with an harquebus across his shoulders and his sword swinging at his side, despite the mud and gore in which he was caked.

"Ladies and gentlemen," he said as he swaggered up the main street. "Boys and girls. Heathen warlocks and godly Christians. It is my great honor to announce to you the arrival of the man of the hour — the one, the only, the unstoppable, Lord Governor Francisco Pizarro!"

As he paused, the crowds looked at him in confusion.

Many eyes darted from his face to the weapons he carried. He could not blame them, given the carnage his weapons inflicted outside the city.

"Accompanied today, in Cuzco, by his closest ally," he continued, walking toward the heart of the town, past temples he had stripped of gold and houses from which aristocrats had supplied small fortunes. "The young prince of a new world. The stripling with more sense than all his elders put together. The governor's good friend and brother in arms, Emperor Manco!"

That last name at least stirred recognition. The crowd began to clap and cheer, some enthusiastically, others reluctantly, most with the attitude so often taken to superiors — interest so mild that it could evaporate in a strong breeze. From what DeSoto had been told, most local aristocrats had either fought in the battle or fled to avoid it. Few here understood the giddy politics surrounding the imperial throne.

DeSoto had never stooped so low as to become an actor, but he knew the importance of putting on a good show. That was why he swaggered and shouted his way into town. But his show was nothing next to that put on by Francisco Pizarro. He had planned this triumphal entry into Cuzco in a matter of moments, seeing immediately how it must be done. The promise of safety and legitimacy alongside the thrill of something new. The gift of riches riding alongside the ever-present threat of violence. A reminder of who now controlled the throne and that they were not the same person who sat upon it.

The disdain DeSoto had seen Pizarro express for these people was hidden behind the veil of dignity. However little the conquistador respected them, the Incas would learn to respect their new masters or face the consequences. It made DeSoto smile inside, even as he too hid his scorn behind victorious grandeur.

As the more reluctant members of the crowd slunk away, perhaps to leave town forever, Manco's supporters came to the fore. And so the conquistadors, fresh from slaughtering the best and brightest of the imperial army, rode into the capital not on a tide of blood but on a wave of adulation.

∽

"It's good to see you again, old friend," Pizarro said, watching embers rise from the fire in the center of the square, ascending like fresh orange stars into the night sky.

"Of course it is," Almagro said. "And not all bad to see you too."

They sat at the edge of the platform on which Cuzco's main temple was built, their legs dangling over the square below. Each had a cup of wine, poured from a bottle Almagro had brought from Panama — carefully selected to celebrate this occasion. Pizarro took a deep gulp of his wine then screwed his face up in distaste.

"I thought you said this was fine wine," he said, glaring at the cup.

"No, I said it was the finest Panama had to offer," Almagro said. "Which is far from the same thing. Though if your brother's response to me packing it is anything to go by, you should be grateful that I didn't down it all in one go on the way here, then lead your reinforcements like lost children around the Americas."

"You've been getting drunk again?" Pizarro looked warily at his friend. Almagro was a good man to have at your side, just as long as you kept him sober. Too many drinks and he became as useless as the next sack of grain.

"Drunkenness wasn't the problem," Almagro said. "Boredom was the problem, drinking was the solution. And don't lecture me about my habits. I've seen you—"

"Enough." Pizarro raised a hand. "As long as you function, how you do it is your business. And you've done a damn fine job of it."

He nodded across the square, where a large number of Almagro's recruits had sat down together, sharpened their blades, and knocked the dents out of their armor.

"They'll do," Almagro agreed. "What about the Incas?"

Pizarro shrugged. "Most of those opposing us scattered. Manco's men are hunting down the rest. After that... Perhaps some more treachery, or perhaps our message has finally been understood. Either way" — he raised his cup — "for now, here's to ruling a whole new world."

"A whole new world." Almagro clinked his cup against Pizarro's. "That's where we are, all right."

CHAPTER FORTY-ONE

Cuzco

As Pizarro looked around the Emperor's palace, he was reminded of years before when he had snuck into the royal palace of the King of Spain and seen Cortez being celebrated for his adventures in the New World. For the first time in his life, he could think about that day without the canker of jealousy poisoning his mind. Yes, his cousin had been celebrated before the whole Spanish court, his wealth and achievements praised by the King himself. But that had all taken place inside the King's palace. Cortez had not had what Pizarro now did — a palace of his own.

He sat on a cushion at the back of the main hall, watching as nobles and administrators lined up before Hernando, giving accounts of themselves and of how they could be useful to the new regime. These were the smart ones — the opportunists who saw that theirs was a Spanish kingdom now and that those who recognized that fact would flourish. Those who resisted, who treated the puppet Manco as the real power here, would soon be sidelined just as surely as those who had fled the battlefield.

They were a strange assortment. Clad in the same outfits

of blocky cotton and feathered fringes that he had seen at Cajamarca, they carried themselves with a busy energy that made them bob and turn as they plotted, explained, argued, and schemed. Was this the way all courts looked to the men who ran them — like so many chickens waiting to have their necks wrung? Or was that just Pizarro showing the desperate mind of his peasant upbringing?

He shuffled on the cushion. What he needed was a chair. Adopting the Emperor's throne would be too much. If word of that got back to Spain then all sorts of questions would be asked. He wouldn't just be the man who had made himself governor — he would become the usurper who had made himself a king. But aside from that throne, the locals seemed to have little concept of what a chair was. He might have to get one of his own men to fashion one for him — hardly the job of a conquering warrior and member of Cuzco's new Christian elite. But these men would remember their humble origins; they would not forget where they had come from and refuse to do useful tasks. If that did happen then they were all in trouble, because there was much dirty work yet to be done.

And here he was, as useless as the dead weight, Old World aristocrats he scorned. Time to get up and get to the business of running an empire.

The room went still as he rose and walked over to stand by Hernando.

"Point out the ones who understand the city best," he said. "I need to start thinking about defenses."

~

"This is the life, eh?" Gonzalo said, standing on an upper tier of the stepped residence he had occupied on Cuzco's main square. "A palace each, pretty servants, and finally some decent food."

"These aren't palaces," Juan said, standing beside him on the smoothly cut stone. "Francisco took the palace, just like he always takes the best of everything."

"Of course they're palaces," Gonzalo said, shaking his head. "They're big, fancy houses for the royal family. What else is a palace?"

"It's one of those," Juan said, pointing at the grand building across the square.

Gonzalo stifled a sigh. A click of his fingers summoned a pretty servant girl in a white tunic, who replaced the empty jugs with fresh ones full of local beer. It turned out that the stuff wasn't entirely awful, or perhaps that a man could get used to it. He prided himself on being pragmatic, and endless beer was endless beer, whether it actually tasted good or he was just imagining that.

As the servant left, he watched the sway of her hips and the tread of delicate feet on cold stone. Maybe he'd find that one again later — she had a charming innocence that he'd love to take. Maybe he'd go for the slightly older one instead, with that wicked twinkle in her eye that said she knew her way around a man's body. Maybe he'd even have both at once. If he could have his own palace and endless beer, then why not that, too?

"I had three of them at once last night," Juan said, apparently reading Gonzalo's mind. His grin returned. "One tending to the stick, one tending to the berries, and one tending to the other two."

"And do you think that sort of thing happens to men who don't have palaces?" Gonzalo said.

"It's never happened to me before." Juan scratched his head. "I'll give you that much."

"There you go then. Palaces. I'd say the ladies love them, but who cares what they love? What matters is that they do as they're told."

The two of them clinked their jugs of beer together and laughed. Then they drank, sharing a moment of silent reflection.

"You know what the best part is?" Juan said.

"There's something better than what you just told me?" Gonzalo asked, contemplating which would be his third serving girl.

"The best part is that we're fighting and drinking our way through a kingdom, and it's all God's work," Juan said, crossing himself.

"I'm not sure Friar Vicente would agree with all that," Gonzalo said. He wasn't a great Biblical scholar, but he knew enough to know that three-serving-girls-at-one-time wasn't high on the divine to-do list.

"Oh, but he does," Juan said. "I checked. He says that as long as we are spreading the good word and Christendom, and as long as we crush heathen practices wherever we see them, then we will be forgiven the sins we commit in that righteous cause. We will receive our reward in heaven."

"You mean that after all this, you'll get three horny angels at once too?" Gonzalo laughed. What was the harm in a little blasphemy if their actions would save them.

Juan stared at the floor for a moment, then he too laughed.

"Why not?" he asked and raised his jug in a toast. "Here's to getting laid in heaven."

CHAPTER FORTY-TWO

The Emperor Manco's Residence, Cuzco

From the corner of the throne room, Cuyoc watched Manco as he received his subjects. They approached him warily, beads rattling on the bracelets at their wrists, uncertain how to behave in this new era. That he was not the emperor of a few months before did not seem to unsettle them — there had been enough upheavals in the preceding years for that not to be a problem. But he was not in the same throne room the emperor had used a few months before, not even in the same palace. That was harder to accept.

Cuyoc was not surprised by the throne room, in a building near the main temple that was much too small for an emperor and his entourage. What surprised her was Manco. The uncertain youth she had thought she saw lurking in Huascar's shadow had been replaced by a confident young man, one who had seized his moment without a hesitation, and who now sat upon his throne as confidently as any ruler before him. He gave judgments, guidance, and assurances to the people petitioning him but did not allow any to linger past the time he could spare. As the afternoon grew late, he had his guards block the doorway and called an end to proceedings. Servants lit a fire in the center of the room as the last petitioners were ushered out. The door was barred, the servants retreated, and the two of them were left alone.

Manco waved her over to stand before the throne.

"I've been trying to decide what to do with you," he said. "I would have favored killing you, given your part in Huascar's downfall."

Cuyoc took a shocked step back. She had never heard him talk this way, never seen such coldness in his eyes.

"I saved you from the bloodshed," she said. "Without me you would have—"

"Spare me the rhetoric." Manco held up his hand, a silver bracelet glinting in the firelight. All his gold was gone, sacrificed to the Spaniards' endless hunger for the yellow metal. "There is no right or wrong here, no debts owed. We each do what we must to protect our own power. I don't know what you had planned for me, but I don't believe you acted purely out of charity."

Cuyoc hesitated. There was truth in what he said, and falsehood as well. She had sought to avert total bloodshed, to save the younger members of her family from the feud tearing the older ones apart. But she had seen value in the boy too, in ensuring there was an heir if anything happened to Atahualpa, in showing that her brother could be merciful in his strength.

"Why not kill me then?" she said. "I'm a symbol of those who stood against you."

"To our people, yes," Manco said. "But to the Spanish you're a symbol of our ability to cooperate. And to Hernando... Well, whatever he has in mind, it brings him as close to my side as any Spaniard. In time, I will need friendly Spaniards, I'm sure."

So many assumptions there, so many plans within plans. If the world had been calmer, Cuyoc would have taken great satisfaction in teasing more out of him, in learning his plans and building her own efforts around them. But right now, she had a more immediate concern.

"What will you do with me then?" she asked.

"I have no intention of marrying you, if that's what you want," Manco said. "Or what you fear. I can't tell, and that's half the reason I should be rid of you. True, you could be very useful, but there are many useful people. And I would rather take Quispe to my bed."

A lecherous smile touched his lips, leaving Cuyoc relieved that it wasn't directed at her.

"I'll need a bigger palace first, though," he said. "A grand new building to mark this new era in the history of our empire. The age of Manco."

"The age of Pizarro, you mean," Cuyoc said, her lips curling.

"I hope to keep the two intertwined," he said. "And for that I need—"

A fist pounded on the door, followed by a voice shouting in Spanish. Guards appeared, dressed in cotton armor and carrying heavy clubs. At a signal from Manco, they slid back the bar and opened the door.

Juan Pizarro stormed in, shouting and waving his sword around. Gonzalo was behind him, a grin on his face and a jug in his hand. The smell of alcohol and stale sweat preceded them.

Fear gripped Cuyoc. Half the Spaniards were rapists and drunks, but the stories she had heard about these two — stories only whispered among the women of Cuzco — indicated that they were the worst. After what had just passed, she didn't trust her brother to save her from such a fate, but she pressed herself up against the throne, where she at least had the small protection Manco's guards offered.

"What does he want?" the Emperor asked, leaning over to whisper in her ear.

Juan's words were a torrent of rage, full of slurs and obscenities that she only half understood. Still, the focus of his anger became clear once she paid attention.

"Quispe," she whispered back, her heart turning to ice at the thought of this man touching the innocent young princess. "He has heard that you intend to marry her. He wants her for himself."

"Who wouldn't?" Manco said.

"What do we do?"

"We count on him." Manco pointed.

Framed by the doorway, Francisco Pizarro stood before the dying light of a grey afternoon. His arms hung at his sides, one by his sword hilt, and he was wearing both breastplate and helmet.

"Enough," he snapped in Spanish. "What damn foolishness is happening now?"

"Quispe," Juan said, turning to stare at his brother. "I demand her as part of my plunder."

Pizarro looked up at Manco.

"And what do you say?" he said.

Manco, still uncertain in his Spanish, nodded to Cuyoc.

"You deal with this," he said. "And remember, I'm not afraid to throw you to the jaguars."

Stepping away from the throne, Cuyoc stood straight and regal, despite the shiver running down her back.

"His divine light the Emperor Manco has chosen his sister Quispe to be his first bride," she said. Part of her felt aghast at passing the poor woman over to this man of cold stone, but better that than the raging inferno of drunken Spaniards.

"Incestuous pigs!" Juan said. "He can't have her. It's filthy, ungodly."

"As opposed to what you do?" Cuyoc let the bile pour out of her; the hatred of so many of these men spewing forth, at last directed at the one who most deserved it. "Rape. Beatings. More rape. Torture. You call that clean?"

"Compared with brother lying with sister?" Juan said. "Hell yes!"

"You sick scum," Cuyoc said, turning her glare upon Pizarro. "Are you any better?"

The look he returned her could have withered a lesser soul away to nothing, but Cuyoc in her fury would not be cowed. Whatever they did to her, she would not stand back and let this happen to her sister.

"Righteousness is between a man and God," Pizarro said. "It is not for you to decide."

"Hah!" Juan said, spittle flying from his lips.

"Nor is it your place to make demands." Francisco turned on his brother. "When you can manage this whole empire without the help of its Emperor, then you can take what he wants." He pointed at Manco. "Until then, get back to whichever whores you've already claimed and exercise a modicum of restraint. Princess Quispe's marriage is for her brother to decide. Its righteousness is between him and God."

Cuyoc translated to Manco as directly as she could. She half expected bitterness to show in his face at the tone Pizarro took, but instead a tight smile appeared.

"Your Majesty agrees, I'm sure," Francisco said. It was a statement, not a question.

"Indeed, I do," Manco said through Cuyoc.

"When you're done here, send her to me," Pizarro said, pointing at Cuyoc. "I have plans, and she is part of them."

As she faltered in her translation, Pizarro turned to look at her.

"You have a long journey ahead of you," he said. "You're going to visit a real court."

He strode away.

Too spent for fear or anger, Cuyoc turned, stony faced, toward her brother.

"You decide Quispe's fate, but he decides mine?" she said.

"I care more about Quispe," Manco said. "I care about you enough only for this piece of advice — make yourself invaluable. In times like this, it's the only way to survive."

CHAPTER FORTY-THREE

Spain

Cuyoc's discomfort at having her fate decided for her was nothing compared to the discomforts that followed. A long journey to the coast, from there by sea up to Panama, and then another overland trek before they even got to the meat of the journey — crossing the Atlantic.

For weeks, she found herself trapped in the confines of a Spanish ship. It had been one thing to see these vessels lined up at the docks, but to travel in one across the open ocean was something else entirely. Her whole world bucked up and down with the Atlantic waves. The timbers creaked, threatening to give in beneath the pressure and drown them all. She could barely keep food down for days on end.

By the time they neared the finish of their voyage, she was at least able to walk about the deck without feeling sick, caught between wonder and terror at a vast, empty world filled with nothing but sea from horizon to horizon. Without Hernando's company, she would have gone mad.

As she stepped off the ship and onto the wharf at Palos de la Fronera, Cuyoc found that her legs still wobbled beneath her. One thing she had looked forward to throughout the journey had been standing on stable ground again, but now she was here, it did not feel as firm as she remembered. It was as if her legs had changed in response to the swaying of the sea and now could not steady themselves without it.

Hernando smiled as he took her arm.

"This will pass," he said in their private language.

Smiling, she leaned over, taking her instability as an excuse to be closer to him. An excuse to herself as well as to others — acknowledging how much he meant to her was something she could barely do within the confines of her mind. The stable, sensible courtier inside her resisted the wild part of her that burned to feel his touch. That part could not be allowed to rule. Not where a Spaniard was concerned.

Not where any man was concerned.

Guiding her to a dockside inn in view of their ship, Hernando found Cuyoc a seat and shelter from the sun. The innkeeper watched Cuyoc with the same wide-eyed curiosity as all the others around them. She knew that she looked different from these people, that she dressed differently from them. But she had not been ready for this. She felt like an insect beneath the gaze of a curious child.

Then Hernando produced a small lump of gold and everything changed. The innkeeper brought her food and drink. People hurried to help unload the boxes, barrels, and sacks that they had brought across the ocean — the goods with which Pizarro hoped to win the King of Spain's favor and be made governor of the lands he had taken.

As the dockers worked and Hernando supervised, Cuyoc sat back and enjoyed the refreshments. She had been given a dish of strange, salty berries and some sliced meat. Anything was a refreshing change after weeks of salt pork and ship biscuits. And the wine... Now she understood why the Spaniards liked it.

As the sun blazed down, Cuyoc watched the men work.

∼

The road to Madrid had left Cuyoc tired, dusty, and saddle sore. Yet as they passed through the gates of the city, she still had time to be amazed.

She had thought that Cuzco was lively, but it was nothing next to this. The closely packed streets were full of people. They shouted, laughed, and whispered in each other's ears. They exchanged goods, coins, and the occasional punch, with armed guards stepping in to break up brawls. Most had skin like that of the Spaniards she had met, but some were pale as chalk, others brown as dried cocoa beans. Many wore drab clothes in grey and brown, but others wore blues, reds, yellows, and greens. One man had bells at the tips of his pointed toes and his many-pointed hat, and he shook them as he danced for the entertainment of others.

And the buildings!

The stonework was not as smooth as in Cuzco, but there were so many buildings and such varied shapes. Instead of straw roofs, buildings were topped with tiles that Hernando told her were made of baked clay. The spires of Christian temples protruded like needles pointing up at their god.

"It's amazing," she said, leaning over in the saddle to talk to Hernando. He had taught her to ride along the way but didn't know how to do so sidesaddle as Spanish ladies did. So she rode like a man, still marveling at the powerful muscles and warm body of the horse between her thighs and at the gentle placidity with which it carried her.

"Wait until you see court," Hernando replied with a grin.

They didn't get into the royal palace that day, but she saw enough to leave her head spinning once more. Outside the gates of the King's residence were gathered dozens of nobles. Their clothes compared to those of the common men as the sun compared with the light of a single candle. The women's dresses flowed and sparkled, decorated with bright silks and dazzling jewels. The men posed in bright doublets and tight hose, sneering down from their horses at the beggars in the gutter.

"How is it that men so richly dressed can live in the same place as such desperate wretches?" she asked.

"The wealthy and the poor," Hernando said with a shrug. "Over here, gold is more than something that shines. It is life and death, starvation and plenty. That is why Francisco is so relentless in his pursuit of it."

Cuyoc nodded. In the rational part of her mind, she understood. This was the way things were here — such vast gaps in wealth, such a focus on gold. It felt like a sort of madness, as if the world had been turned upside down, values twisted on their heads. Even as she contemplated it, striving to understand how she should act to fit in, she felt dizziness at the distorted way these people lived.

In her heart, she shrank away from it, appalled as she watched armed and armored guards beat a beggar and then drag him away. Wind swirled dust across the cobbles, and even the blood that had dripped from his nose was hidden. But that dreadful gap between rich and poor remained, in a world where wealth was everything.

CHAPTER FORTY-FOUR

The Royal Palace, Madrid

King Charles was one of the strangest men Cuyoc had ever met. It was not just his plethora of titles — King Charles I of Spain, Emperor Charles V of the Holy Roman Empire, Duke of Limburg, Count of Zutphen, and two dozen more the herald had listed as they arrived. It was the way he looked and the way he sat. Even by Spanish standards his appearance was odd — his skin pale, his nose long, his beard unable to conceal his unnaturally jutting jaw. Yet there was a friendly curiosity in his eyes as he watched them approach the throne, bow and curtsy in line with the protocols they had been taught, and finally stand waiting for him to speak. As he did so, he sat awkwardly in his throne, as if he were never entirely comfortable — at odds with his body, not with the rites of court.

Beside the King sat his wife, Isabella of Portugal, in a dress of purple and gold. Her smile was one of careful calculation as she cast an evaluating gaze over the new arrivals. A woman finding her way in a world run by men. Cuyoc was pleased to see a kindred spirit.

This place, at last, was something familiar — the sort of

environment she had spent her life preparing for. The architecture might be strange, with its high ceiling and tiled floor; the people dressed in oddly shaped clothes and staring at her like she was a foreign bird brought forth to entertain; the words comprehensible thanks only to months of learning from Hernando. Yet still, this was a court, a place of overt rituals and covert schemes, and that was a place in which Cuyoc could excel.

Hernando, on the other hand, was a little lost. He was not making crass errors as some of his brothers might, but formality did not suit him any more than the overly tight doublet he had bought the day before — black, to match that summer's fashions. For a moment, she feared that he had forgotten the rules for introductions, explained to them only minutes before, and there was an awkward pause after he was presented to the King. But then he mastered himself.

"Your Majesty," he said, "may I present Princess Cuyoc, sister of the Emperor Manco of the Incas."

"A pleasure to meet you, Your Highness." Charles started to rise from his chair, winced, and sank back down. No one reacted.

"And you, Your Majesty," Cuyoc said, curtsying even lower than before. It would have been easier in a Spanish dress, designed as they were for this life. Hernando had even bought her one; a thing of stunning red and yellow that had taken her eye as they explored the markets and shops. But today she was to play the part of the exotic princess, the foreign wonder brought back from Francisco Pizarro's new lands. Just as much as the golden statues and caged jaguars that had followed them into the room, her presence was a gift for the

King and a spectacle to dazzle the court.

"Do you speak much Spanish?" Charles asked, then shook his head and laughed. "As if you could answer me if you did not."

The courtiers dutifully joined him in a brief, low chuckle, all making sure to show just the right level of appreciation for the monarch's wit.

"As if Your Majesty would ask if he did not suspect the answer," Cuyoc said. "I grew up in the imperial court, have served as adviser to three rulers, and have never known one to gaze with such sharp awareness around his court."

"And I have never known an ambassador who did not flatter," the King said.

"It is our job," Cuyoc said. "And our deepest pleasure."

She curtsied again, and as she did so raised an eyebrow ever so slightly. Beside her, Hernando tapped his finger against his costume, and the rest of the courtiers held their breath.

But Cuyoc knew she had judged her man right.

King Charles laughed, and the rest followed.

"I think Pizarro has tricked me," he said. "You sound as if you have spoken our language from a young age."

"I had an excellent tutor," Cuyoc said, nodding toward Hernando.

"Then we are grateful to you, master Pizarro," the King said, looking at Hernando. "Thanks to you, not just beauty but charm has been added to my court in the form of this young woman."

There was a flutter of applause from the courtiers, who seemed not to notice the slight narrowing of the Queen's eyes.

"Give me no credit," Hernando said. "Princess Cuyoc's charm is of her own making, her beauty God's, and her presence a wonder to all who meet her."

This time the court's approval came as a murmur of softly spoken words. The Queen's gaze narrowed in on Cuyoc.

"Such a pleasure to meet you," she said, her tone not matching the words.

"And you, Your Majesty." Cuyoc made sure to curtsy extra low.

"But tell me, what else have you brought from our faraway lands?" the Queen asked.

Drawing Cuyoc aside, Hernando ushered forwards a line of servants carrying gold, jewelry, strange plants, and stranger animals. Half a dozen of them warily pushed the pair of caged jaguars forwards.

"Wonderful!" Charles said, looking at the gifts and then back at Cuyoc. "Now you must tell me all about this new land of ours — this land of Inca."

CHAPTER FORTY-FIVE

The Private Chambers of King Charles I

Sweat beading his brow, Hernando walked down the corridor between four armed and armored guards. He had no weapon of his own, no armor beyond the satin doublet gifted to him by the Queen, cloth so yellow it was almost gold showing through the slashes of the blue sleeves. He straightened the soft matching hat and tried to calm his racing thoughts.

Why did the King want to see him alone? Was this something that often happened? Was it a good sign or a bad one? How was he meant to behave?

He wished he had Cuyoc with him. She could have made sense of this. She would have known how he should act. But she had not been there when the guards came for him, and they had given him no time to linger. When the King of Spain asks for you, you come that very moment.

The guards stopped at a pair of double doors reinforced with elaborate iron moldings of lions and birds in flight. They knocked, and on receiving a brief answer, pushed open one door, then stepped aside. Hernando was pushed through, then the door swung shut behind him.

He found himself in a large receiving room. The table in

the center held wine, cheese, and sliced meat. Beyond that were large padded couches in front of a set of windows that filled most of the wall, their shutters open to let in the morning light. As Hernando stared, he realized that they weren't just shutters — the windows were glazed, more glass than he remembered ever seeing in one place, and those leaded panes had also been pushed open.

King Charles sat alone, sprawled out on one of the couches, wearing only a shirt and hose.

"Good to see you, Hernando," he called across the room. "Come, take a seat. Bring the wine with you as you pass."

It appeared that servants and courtiers did not always surround the King of Spain. As instructed, Hernando picked up the wine, poured a cup and passed it to the King, then perched on a seat across the window from the monarch.

"Relax," Charles said. "Pour a drink for yourself."

Hernando feared that anything he added to his trembling stomach would reappear moments later, but he didn't dare say that to the King or disobey his will. He poured another cup, forced himself to sit back, and took a sip of the most excellent wine he had ever tasted.

"I've been wondering for some time about taking a new mistress," Charles said, almost causing Hernando to choke on his drink. "I love Isabella dearly, but variety is the spice of life. Lately my tastes have bent toward the exotic. Tell me, would the Princess Cuyoc be amenable to becoming my mistress?"

Staring at the King, Hernando struggled to untangle his reactions. He knew that affairs were something nobles did, but he had never expected them to be addressed so matter-of-factly. Even as he processed the words, he recognized that a request from his King was not really a request, but a politely phrased order. This was not what he wanted for Cuyoc — to become one more novelty in the royal bedchamber. But then, what he wanted for Cuyoc could never really happen, because it was the two of them together, forever, and their very different lives stood in the way of that.

Would Cuyoc even allow the Spanish King to make use of her in this way? Hernando had no idea, but he knew that for her to say 'no' could bring down terrible consequences upon her, as well as damage the good favor in which Charles viewed the Pizarro expedition. It could wreck Francisco's chances of being made governor — the whole reason he had sent them here.

More than ever, Hernando wanted Cuyoc by his side to show him a way out of this.

And then he saw one.

"I'm afraid that the princess is already married," he said. What was one lie compared with the things he had done in the Americas?

"To whom?" the King said.

"To me." It was a desperate, panicked answer, but the only one Hernando could imagine giving.

"Since when?" The King narrowed his eyes. "Why was I not told?"

"It is a secret," Hernando said, thoughts flying wildly as he tried to cover for himself. Was the King a romantic? Could that get him out of this? "We are very much in love, but the situation in your new lands is tense, and so we could not be married there. But on arriving in Spain we found a discrete minister and were married in the eyes of God and his church."

"Hmm." Charles stroked his beard. "A shame. Taking a married woman as a mistress is too complicated. Breaking your union would need the Pope's blessing, and I cannot afford to spend his favors so lightly. Ah well."

He drank his wine while Hernando sat, a ball of unbearable tension, waiting to see how badly he had harmed his relations with the King. If he had brought another Incan girl across the ocean then he could have offered her in Cuyoc's place. The thought was distasteful, but kings were not men to be easily denied, and softening the blow might save his position. Yet he had no such girl. Was a king's disappointment about to bring all of their plans crashing down?

"You are a funny lot, you Pizarros." Charles smiled and pulled a letter from the pile of cushions against which he was resting. "When you see what you want, you don't let anything stop you, do you?"

"Nothing but God and Your Majesty," Hernando said, bowing his head. Was that smile a good sign, or was the King enjoying the thought of vengeance for being slighted?

"I've been reading the letter you brought from your brother," the King said. "I admire his brazenness, both in dealing with the natives and in making his requests of me. Such daring, when not turned to begging a king or marrying a princess, could carve out great new territories for my kingdom in this new world of ours. I shall grant your brother his governorship of the Inca lands and the rights attached to it. I expect great things from both of you over there."

"Thank you, Your Majesty." No longer needing to hide his feelings, Hernando grinned as wide as the heavens. "And Diego de Almagro? Will he be granted a position too?"

"I think not," the King said. "Your brother makes a compelling argument for a single point of authority, one man from whom all decisions in that region can flow. That man will be him."

It was a day full of surprises. Not having read the sealed letter, Hernando had assumed that he was serving his brother's long-standing agreement to share their gains with Almagro. Instead, Francisco was keeping all the power for himself.

Hernando wanted to think it through, to consider the implications, but all he could think of was Cuyoc. He had spared her from the King's bed, but he had done so with a lie, a lie that would doubtless now filter out through the court as gossip. What would she think of his presumptuous story? Would she still be willing to speak to him when he had risked her honor in this way?

"Let us celebrate your achievements," the King said, wincing as he leaned forwards to pour the wine himself.

Hernando raised his cup in a toast and then his voice in conversation. But his mind was elsewhere.

CHAPTER FORTY-SIX

The Ship the Santa Christopher, the Atlantic Ocean

Perhaps it was a change in the season, perhaps experience at sea, or perhaps the uplifting thought that she was returning home. Whatever the reason, Cuyoc was finding the return across the Atlantic far more pleasant than the voyage to Spain. Her stomach barely churned at all, and she had been standing steady within minutes of leaving port. With the coast of Spain now hidden behind the horizon, she felt safe and secure in the thought that she would soon be back in the empire and that Hernando was here to protect her along the way.

She could tell that he couldn't hear her coming. Even when he tried to mask his response, to let her think that she had won their game by creeping up on him, she saw the telltale shift of his head. But this time he stood unmoving, staring out to sea.

The ship creaked as it tilted on a wave. A fine salt spray hit her face as she joined him at the rail, leaning close before she spoke.

"Thank you," she said quietly and then paused to enjoy watching surprise and delight cross his face at her presence. "As you promised, you are bringing me safely home."

"Of course." His smile faltered, his expression growing serious. "There's something I have to tell you."

Concern rose in a wave as strong as those lifting their vessel. Something had gone amiss in Spain. Were they returning to danger? Had they left it behind, only for it to pursue them?

"I had to lie to the King," Hernando said. "About you..."

He told his story. The private meeting with the King. Charles's desire to take her to his bed, a desire that sickened Cuyoc even as she heard it dismissed. The foreign King with his jutting jaw, pained joints, and jealous wife was not what she wanted from a husband, never mind a lover.

Then came the explanation of how Hernando got her out of this. He stared down at the waves, red-faced and unwilling to look her in the eye.

"I'm sorry," he said. "It was all I could think to do."

Cuyoc grappled with her feelings. It was all she could do to keep from grinning. The thought of marrying Hernando was one she had harbored in her heart of hearts. Though the whole thing had been a deception, a swift lie for politics, to hear him speak the possibility made her feel giddy. Then there was the absurdity of the whole situation, a ridiculousness that made her want to laugh aloud.

But there was something serious here as well. A lie to a king was a dangerous thing, and there was no way that this one could remain a secret forever.

"It was worse than presumptuous," she said. "It was dangerous."

"What do you think I have been brooding on here?" Hernando said. "Word will get back to King Charles that we have returned to Peru as two separate people, not the married couple I told him we are. We cannot trust my brother's comrades with secrecy around this, never mind trust your brother's court. And when the King finds out about my lie, he will have us both executed."

He turned to look at her, tears welling in the corners of his eyes.

"I'm so sorry," he said. "You are the most wonderful thing to me. More beautiful than all the art in all the royal palaces of the world. More amazing than the jungles and cities of your home. I have endangered your life. I can see only one way out, and to suggest it makes me feel as great a scoundrel as my brothers."

"I too see only one way out," she said, still fighting not to smile. "It is certainly an imposition and may anger both our families, but if you have been a scoundrel it is in creating this problem, not solving it."

"I know," Hernando hung his head. "I'll try to think of another way around this. We have the whole voyage back."

"Leaving it so long would undermine the story you gave the King," she said, still mock serious. "We should get to it now, so that all on this voyage may see us as married."

Hernando nodded.

"There's a friar travelling with us to join Vicente," he said. "I will speak with him, beg to do this quietly and back-date the papers. I only care that it is done right in God's eyes, but it is the King's gaze that will matter to others."

Of course, he was right. The look of this could not be

about their feelings, or even about right or wrong. It was about the look of it.

She expected him to leave then, to fetch the friar and get the thing done. Instead he looked around and, seeing no one watching this corner of the deck, knelt before her.

"Cuyoc, will you marry me?" he asked, a nervous smile lifting the corners of his mouth.

"Did we not just decide this?" she asked, confused and wondering why her husband-to-be was not standing to talk with her.

"This is how Spanish men propose," Hernando said. "Humbling ourselves as a sign of love and admiration. So, please, before someone catches me in this moment of heartfelt foolishness, will you marry me?"

"Of course," she said. Overcome by an excitement that, for once in her life, she could not suppress, she flung her arms around him and whispered in his ear. "I don't care that it began as a lie. I can think of no better husband in all the world."

His face lit up, glowing like a golden sun.

Both smiling as wide as they had ever smiled in their lives, the conquistador and the princess set out to find the priest.

By nightfall, they were wed.

CHAPTER FORTY-SEVEN

Cuzco

Juan drew his dagger, flung it twirling into the air, and caught it by the sides of the blade as it fell. Then he did it again, and again, and again, watching the blade spin a little higher each time until it hit the ceiling of the waiting room and fell with a clatter to the floor. Sweeping it up, he thrust the blade back in its sheath and looked for something else to distract him. Anything to take his mind off the tedious wait for his audience with Francisco. Bad enough that he had to go through this shit to get what he wanted, but now he had to wait first.

The voices in the throne room were growing louder. The two men on guard — both members of the original expedition to Cajamarca — glanced at each other and then at him. One shifted his pike awkwardly from one hand to the other, so that he could scratch the sunburnt side of his face.

"What?" Juan said. "You thinking I might walk in and interrupt that shit? Let the bastards shout each other down. It's their damn business, not ours."

"Sorry, Juan." The sunburnt guard, Jose, gave him a stupid sheepish grin. "It's just, you know..."

"Piss on 'you know,'" Juan said. "We fight when he asks us

to fight. We guard when he asks us to guard. We mind our own business when others are talking. And when we get an hour off we get to drink our rewards. That's the job we signed up for, so don't give me your little girl smile and your 'you know.'"

The other guard laughed. Then they were all laughing. They'd been through too much together — too many battles, too many whores, too many casks of wine — for friction to build because of a few words.

The past year had seen enough tension to last them a lifetime. First the fight for control of this empire. Then the long wait while Hernando travelled to Spain and back, while they clung on amidst recalcitrant rebels and pompous nobles, trying not to let it slip away. Waiting for reinforcements, and for word on whether they could keep what they had taken.

Now Hernando was back with good news. Juan had seen the pressure seep out of Francisco as he heard what King Charles had to say, and as he read the list of supplies travelling down from Panama. But there had been other news too — news that pleased Juan less, and that had brought him here today.

The door burst open and Almagro stormed out. Halfway across the entrance hall he looked back, pointing into the throne room.

"Don't think I don't know what you're up to, Francisco," he yelled. "This might come from the King, but we all know where it started. I'll have my equal share, or I'll burn this hell hole down."

He stormed away.

"My turn," Juan said.

"Actually..." Jose nodded toward a group of Incas coming in off the street. At their head was Manco; the little prick looking smug and self-satisfied as always.

"Oh no, they don't." Juan walked halfway across the throne room and was opening his mouth to speak when Francisco, who sat on a stool at the foot of the great stone seat, held up a hand.

"After this," the older Pizarro said.

Face twisted with fury, Juan stepped aside to let Manco, this child who thought he was an emperor, take his place.

"Governor Pizarro," Manco said, not bowing his head.

"Your Highness," Pizarro said, not rising from his seat. Their voices echoed around the cavernous room, stripped of all its decorations for the treasure hoard.

"There has been more trouble," Manco said. "Two of your soldiers attacked one of my nobles."

"As I understand it, your noble and his men tried to throw my soldiers out of a temple," Pizarro said. "My men are allowed everywhere, Your Highness, so unless I misheard them, my men were not at fault."

Manco remained expressionless, but the courtiers behind him frowned and muttered to each other. Juan was tempted to draw his sword and run them through, to see if that drew a reaction from the Emperor.

"Tensions are high," Manco said. "My people feel put upon by the unexpected marriage of my sister and your brother."

"And how do you feel about it?" Francisco Pizarro was equally expressionless, but Juan knew that look — it came when his brother wanted to do one thing and did another for the sake of his plans. It wasn't something Juan could do, however often he saw it done. That was why he followed Francisco.

That and gold.

"I feel that I have lost an important bargaining chip," Manco said. "And that this leaves me unable to spend more to manage current tensions."

"Of course." Pizarro whistled and Zárate came in through a side door. The clerk looked displeased, as he so often did these days. His clerical work had left him lumbered with carrying important messages; a task he had drunkenly told Juan he considered beneath him.

"Governor?" Zárate said.

"Spread the word, we're having a command meeting this evening. About discipline."

"Yes, Governor."

The clerk disappeared the same way he came in.

"Thank you, Governor," Manco said.

He turned his back and walked toward the doors with his entourage behind him.

"One more thing, Manco," Pizarro said.

Juan saw the moment of hesitation as Manco chose between disobeying Francisco and being seen ordered around in front of his men. The governor glared as Juan snorted with laughter.

"Yes, Governor?" Manco paused, not walking any farther but not turning back.

"That's the last time you use Hernando's marriage as an excuse," Pizarro said.

Juan watched in amazement. His brother hadn't offered a threat, but the Incas acted as if he had. They cowered, Manco mumbled an agreement, and then they scurried away. How did Francisco manage that?

Once they were all gone, Pizarro stood from his seat.

"All right, Juan," he said. "Tell me what you want."

Then Juan remembered — he was mad at his brother. Mad at two of his brothers, and this was one of them.

"How come Hernando gets to take his princess and I don't?" Juan demanded. "I've worked as hard as him, taken as many risks as him, killed more savages than him. So why does he get a prize and I don't?"

"The situations aren't the same," Pizarro said, clear and calm.

"They're both heathen princesses. What's the difference?"

"These aren't two interchangeable bars of gold." Pizarro took a deep breath and rubbed the bridge of his nose as he came closer. He laid a brotherly hand on Juan's shoulder. "They are sisters of an emperor, pieces in the great game we are playing."

"Well I asked for my game piece first, so why am I the one left holding my pawn?" Juan shrugged off the hand.

"Enough, Juan."

"No, not enough. I've been a good soldier. I've done what you asked. I've stuck with you through all this, across oceans and jungles and rivers full of those bastard biting fishes. So why don't I get mine?"

"Because." Francisco stood.

Juan felt his feet leave the ground as his brother slammed him back against the wall, arm across his throat, choking the breath out of him. His head hit the stones and lights danced in front of his eyes, but none of that was as shocking as the fury on his brother's face.

"Because, you arrogant, short-sighted, prick-waving, whore-addled little wart, there is an empire at stake. An empire richer and vaster than we could even have imagined back in those dust bowls we called home. And even if it were nothing but two hovels and a ditch I would still cling to it with every ounce of my strength and every scrap of cunning I can muster, because I have endured too long and fought too hard to let the Pizarro name sink back into dirt and obscurity.

"As a child, you had our mother and your father and a full belly. I had hunger and filth and being kicked through the streets. Everything I have, I have earned with my two hands and my one mind, and I will not lose it to the whims of others. Not for you, not for Manco, not for Almagro, not for the King and the Pope nor all the angels in heaven."

He dropped the stunned Juan, who lay gasping on the floor, crossing himself at his brother's final blasphemy.

"We earned this," Francisco said, waving around him at the throne room, the palace, and the city beyond. "But there is more to be done if we are to make this empire ours. And we will make it ours, come salvation or damnation."

Francisco walked to the window and drew back the shades. The sun was setting and a crowd had gathered in the square. He motioned for Juan to join him.

Juan rose, resentment still bubbling in the back of his mind. Sometimes he just had to obey.

As he approached the window, he saw the town square of Cuzco. The heathen temple. His palace. Gonzalo's. Manco's. And above it all the glowing ball of the sun, sinking toward the horizon. If he were Gonzalo, he might have said something smart about it all. If he were Hernando, something poetic.

"Our brother's returned," Francisco said, pointing down into the square.

A golden litter was carried to the steps of the main square, then lowered. Hernando and Cuyoc emerged. The crowd faced them, judging them. Weighing this new couple. The fusion of the past and the present. The beauty and the power. The Inca and the Spanish.

Hernando took Cuyoc's arm under his and took strong strides forward into the square. The sea of Incas parted. Spanish guards moved closer, sensing danger and wishing to protect a Pizarro.

But slowly, whispers in the crowd began. An old woman turned to her neighbor, putting words in her ear. Then another. Then a young man called out into the twilight sky. It was a high-pitched, squeak of a call. It was triumphant and exclamatory. It was applause. It was Incan.

A smile spread across Cuyoc's face at the noise. Hernando placed his other hand on top of her arm and continued his long strides across the square to his palace. Soon, other shrill cries launched up into the sky above them. The crescendo produced a cacophony of screams and words and adulation.

The crowd had spoken. The marriage of the Incan princess and the Spanish invader had been accepted. At least, accepted by the natives of Cuzco Square.

"Damn that pretentious fop," Juan said to himself as he continued looking down from Francisco's window. "And his royal taste."

Behind Juan, Francisco Pizarro had long since walked

away from the scene. Francisco sat at the foot of the empty throne, deep in thought.

Juan turned back to the window to see Hernando and Cuyoc slip into their palace and out of sight. The cries from the crowd slowed then ceased, and the market went back to the normal business of the day. Like ripples in a pond that fade into calm water.

"Those poor bastards," Juan said. "They have no idea what happens now."

Made in the USA
Lexington, KY
07 August 2018